T0161039

The Dedicated Dancer

Annie Taylor: The Woman Who Conquered
Niagara Falls in a Barrel

MARCY BOWSER

Clovercroft Publishing

This book is dedicated to my husband, Sam, my daughter Julie, and loving family; without their help and support I couldn't have written or published this book. Also, to Aunt Arlene Irvin, whose encouragement and curiosity helped me finish this book.

The Dedicated Dancer

Published by Clovercroft Publishing, Franklin, Tennessee
www.clovercroftpublishing.com

Edited by Robert Irvin

Cover and Interior Design by Suzanne Lawing

ISBN: 978-1-950892-62-4

Printed in the United States of America

Contents

Preface

Annie Taylor lived in the Victorian age. A double standard existed between men and women during this time and was widely practiced and quite well known. She was well educated for a woman of her era. She could speak foreign languages, she was educated in dancing, music, and physical culture, and she had a depth of study in science.

Annie was the first person to go over Niagara Falls' Horseshoe Falls in a barrel—and live. Many came to see her on the day she attempted her feat; the odds seemed totally against her. At least as far as the public was concerned.

According to Annie's personal account, which I have drawn from for this book, she was 46 years old when she went over the Falls, and did so on her birthday. From her account, she was born October 24, 1855; from other accounts, she was born in 1838. She went over the Falls on that birthday, October 24, 1901—so this was either her 46th or 63rd birthday. Quite the difference, I agree. I had to do research and then make my choice for this book.

Why did I undertake this project? There are two reasons. One, I felt Annie had pretty much received a raw deal in the public eye as a daredevil. Second, she seemed way ahead of her time. Annie Taylor's marriage to one S.D. (Samuel) Taylor has been disputed by a few. But I have no reason to doubt this; I know she was married to a Taylor as my grandmother was a Taylor and a cousin by marriage to Annie. My grandmother said she had many cousins in Michigan, and the family had been mortified by some of Annie's actions—especially the choice to go over Horseshoe Falls in a barrel.

Grandma didn't want anyone to know she was related to Annie (even though not by blood but through marriage); the family had basically disowned her. I actually thought Annie was pretty cool.

Grandma didn't want anyone to know she was related to Annie (even though not by blood but through marriage); the family had basically disowned her. She told me this when I was a girl of about 10. I actually thought Annie was pretty cool. My grandmother had not even told my mom or my aunt, it seems, because I asked my mom about Annie's Falls plunge after my grandmother had passed, and Mom seemed rather shocked at the revelation.

For this book, I'm going to make the assumption that Annie was born in 1838. Records, then, would also show that she married at 18, in 1856. Samuel and Annie had a baby boy together, but this child died very young. My research also showed that Samuel died on July 6, 1863, just three days after the last day of battle, and from wounds suffered in, the famous Battle of Gettysburg. Samuel was buried in Branchport Cemetery, Branchport, Yates County, New York.[1] Annie's older brother, Delano James Edson, passed away on July 13, 1863;

he also died from wounds suffered in Gettysburg and also was buried in Branchport Cemetery, Branchport.[2] There is nothing more tragic than the loss of a child or spouse. For Annie to have endured both in such a short span of time, and at such a young age, seems incomprehensible to me. On top of that, she lost her older brother within days as well. And, as we will see, her parents died when she was still a girl.

Annie would rebound, though. And for her day and age, she was quite the traveler. Traveling—especially for a woman by herself, unescorted in any way—in the 1880s was not only risky but also a bit scandalous. Annie's family and friends were not on board with the idea of a widow traveling by herself.

And yet, travel she did.

In her memoirs Annie writes about traveling from New York to Cuba in October 1880. Later she traveled to Galveston, Texas, and then on to Austin and San Antonio, Texas. She left Cuba after staying there about a month. Because single women rarely traveled alone at that time, I believe it is unlikely she was by herself—but if she did begin her travels alone, an attractive widow would not be by herself for long. And yet, it would have been scandalous for Mrs. Annie Taylor to divulge any facts concerning a new relationship developed while traveling.

Because single women rarely traveled alone at that time, I believe it is unlikely she was by herself—but if she did begin her travels alone, an attractive widow would not be by herself for long.

Cuba was highly favored by American businessmen at that time. It was a developing country and, with its bustling seaports, a gateway to South America. Cuba was, and is, a semitropical paradise, average temperatures ranging from 70 to 81 degrees Fahrenheit. It is an island nation with more than five thousand species of flowers and a variety of beautiful tropical birds. It would have also been somewhat dangerous for a widow to stay there for a month by herself as Cuba's wars of independence from Spain (which lasted about thirty years) were going on at the time. Either way, alone or with someone, it had to be an exciting place for a woman who had grown up in Auburn, New York and never traveled any farther than to a teaching school in New Albany, New York, or to Bay City, Michigan, with her new husband.

Her travel had to be expensive as well as dangerous. Even if she had the stamina and nerve to travel by herself, she was a poor widow, a schoolteacher. How could she afford it, I wondered. Either her husband left her some money or someone paid her fare (either her friends or a suitor). From her own words: "One stormy day in October, 1880, [I] took a ship from New York for Cuba, and after a month's stay . . . " She went on to write that she then took a ship to Galveston. She took the railroad from Galveston to Austin, and then traveled by stagecoach to San Antonio. There she met up with friends, the Kingsburys.[3]

My research for this book lasted eight years, beginning in 2012; I found some fascinating history. I researched as much as possible the destinations Annie said she visited. I did my best to describe these destinations in as historically accurate a manner as I could. Our country was a fascinating and colorful place in the late 1800s; it was bulging from growth and evolving quickly with all the development and change.

After studying the timeline in her memoirs, a thirteen-page booklet, I decided to write this account of her life as an historical fiction novel. A number of aspects of Annie's life can only be supposed. Thus, most of the characters in her travels in this book are fictional. Annie's memoirs left much to the imagination. That is why I have chosen the historical fiction approach and not a biographical one.

There is no way to know who Annie shared time with in her lengthy travels. Therefore, her lover in this book, Calvin (who was a professional gambler), is fictional. A professional gambler was a respected occupation in those times! But it was also a dangerous occupation. There wasn't a lot of law enforcement back then, especially in America's Southwest. The dress for professional gamblers, from my research, was as I described in this book.

> A professional gambler was a respected occupation in those times! But it was also a dangerous occupation. There wasn't a lot of law enforcement back then.

The other fictional characters in her travels were Mrs. Broom, Mr. Wiggins, Al, Pam, Ezekiel Good, and Harry the con man in Chattanooga, Tennessee. Ms. Amanda, at the Swannanoa Hotel in Asheville, North Carolina also is fictional, as are Henry and Ellen, the dance instructors in New York City. Annie's best friend, Emily, in Auburn, New York, also is fictional.

Finally, I have added some extra elements in the back of this book that I hope you enjoy, including a timeline of Annie's travels and a picture of what Normal School (where Annie received her Teaching Degree) looked like in those days. The first item I present there, however, is from her self-written booklet about her trip over the Falls, which makes for fascinating reading.

I truly hope you enjoy reading this book as much as I did writing it.

Marcy Bowser
Newark, Ohio
July 2020

CHAPTER 1

Childhood Gone

It was October 24, 1901, very early in the morning. Annie was pondering the life-changing task ahead of her. Could she survive?

Would she survive a plunge over Niagara Falls? Cold, swiftly moving morning waters lie before her. Her mind raced backward. . . . She had survived so many other events and catastrophes in which she thought she might not . . .

Annie Edson had a strong but carefree childhood. She grew up in Auburn, New York on the banks of Owasco Lake. She lived in the city in the winter, where she was enrolled in a city school, and her family lived and worked on an outlying farm in the summer, where she attended what was called a district school. She adored her father, Merick Edson. Merick operated a mill on Owasco Outlet between the city of Auburn and Owasco Lake, New York. After a competing woolen mill in Auburn took away his waterpower, he became a farmer and the family lived on what was known as the Reister Farm, located southwest of Auburn.

Annie's father was the center of her life, her security, her strength.[4] He adored Annie; she was his little daredevil way back then, fearless and strong, afraid of nothing. He loved his boys, but Annie was the apple of his eye. He tried to be strict with her, as he understood a different standard existed for men and women, but it was very difficult for him at times.

> He adored Annie; she was his little daredevil way back then, fearless and strong, afraid of nothing. He loved his boys, but Annie was the apple of his eye.

Sometimes, for Merick, it was just fun to watch Annie and her acrobatics. She was always showing her daddy how she could do cartwheels or jump from limb to limb on trees. Sometimes she would pull other stunts and he would scold her, but then when he saw his little Annie looking downcast he would pick her up and toss her in the air and catch her. He could not stand to see Annie sad.

Her mother, Lucretia, was always fussing at Annie to be a young lady, but Annie just didn't have it in her. She would try to please her mom, but then she would take off running, trying to keep up with her two older brothers. (Annie also had an older sister and three younger brothers; sadly, she had three siblings that died at birth.) Annie found she could keep up with her brothers if she really pushed herself, but when she saw her dad or mom watching she would slow down. Merick could not help but see the humor in the situation. Annie would come in with dirty face and hands and her mother would gently scold her, telling her how she must act more like a young lady. Merick would smile at Annie and say to his wife, "Lucretia, you may as well tell the wind to stop blowing as to try to control this child's nature."[5] That's when her mother would get really wound up. Her father would wink at Annie and then sneak off to where things were a little more peaceful. In all fairness, Annie loved her mom very much as well. Her mother seemed such a gentle soul, one not built for the challenges of the rugged nineteenth century.

> Merick would smile at Annie and say to his wife, "Lucretia, you may as well tell the wind to stop blowing as to try to control this child's nature."

At 11, Annie survived losing her dear father. Then, without warning, just a few years later, her mother—who bore ten children—also died. (Records do not clearly indicate what her parents died from; speculation does not serve a useful purpose.) The grief young Annie felt was almost unbearable; first her father, than her mother. It became difficult for her to speak of her loss or write about it without choking up. She and her two older brothers were assigned by the state to a guardian who chose to send them to a seminary school for orphans.[6] Annie was still so very young and had no one, really, to guide her to womanhood.

Annie would have periods of deep sadness. There were so many times she needed her mother, and she had so many questions. Most of all, though, she missed her mother's gentle touch when she kissed all of her children good night at bedtime.

A short time later, Annie was sent away to school, away from her siblings, except for, perhaps, a chance meeting with one of her older brothers at school. She felt as though she had completely lost her family. Due to the indifferent—some might say stoic—societal attitude shown to widows and orphans at the time, along with those who had suffered immense loss, a person was not to look back, only forward; that was the only way to recover from loss.

Lingering over one's grief was considered a sign of weak mind and weak will. Those who wallowed in self-pity were viewed with contempt. It was in this environment that Annie moved into the later years of her schooling.

CHAPTER 2

Brief Bliss

A few years later, she met him: Samuel D. Taylor.[7] He was so handsome; his eyes twinkled when he smiled. She could not believe he fell in love with her: plain little Annie from seminary school! He was her hero. How excited she was to find herself marrying at the young age of 18!

She remembered the first time she met him. He had come to visit his sister, Jennie, her roommate, Miss Jennie Taylor, "a fine and accomplished scholar."[8] Jennie was Annie's close friend at the seminary school where they lived, in Charlotteville, New York. On that first meeting they had lunch together, Jennie, Samuel, and herself. When Annie first met him, she was touched at the gentle way he addressed his sister and the concern he showed for her wellbeing. When Samuel looked at Annie, she had feelings she never felt before. He asked, "Do you have any brothers or sisters here?" When she replied that her two older brothers were at the school, but that she rarely saw them, he asked, "Do you have any other family?" "Yes, I have three younger brothers and one older sister, but they are with relatives," Annie said.[9] "How old were you when you were sent here?" he asked. She answered that she was 14, that the family guardian had sent them to continue their education.

"You are a strong girl, Annie. That impresses me," Samuel said. Indeed he was quite taken with her. She was younger than Jennie, but she seemed extremely mature for her age. Not mature in a worldly way, mature in her acceptance of her lot in life. She had such a positive attitude about being sent to seminary school, and from what his sister Jennie told him, and from her attitude, Samuel could see she was making the most of this opportunity for education.

> She was younger than Jennie, but she seemed extremely mature for her age. Not mature in a worldly way, mature in her acceptance of her lot in life.

Annie was a pretty young lady with smooth skin and curly hair. As Samuel got to know her better, he found out some other things. She was smart, energetic, and a bit of a daredevil. His visits to the seminary became more frequent, and longer. Any time he could spend with Annie was precious.

When it came time for Annie to graduate, Samuel couldn't bear the thought of her being on her own. He didn't know if her older brothers or sister would take her in or not. Like many young people, they were wrapped up in their own challenges and careers and getting a foothold in life.

Annie looked forward to Samuel's visits. He was the one bright spot in her week; she couldn't wait until he arrived each week. She remembered her first kiss from him. It was so sweet. There were some intangible moments she wished she could hold on to forever; that was one of them. When Samuel pulled out a ring and asked her to marry him, she almost couldn't breathe. He wanted her to be his wife—little Annie Edson, the orphan, thinking about being wedded to such a handsome young man.

He wanted her to be his wife—little Annie Edson, the orphan, thinking about being wedded to such a handsome young man.

Their wedding was simple. Jennie was there, and Samuel's parents. Her brothers came with their girlfriends, her older sister came with her husband, and her aunt attended as well. Extended family members came and seemed happy for both of them. The vows exchanged were traditional, the wedding short. Annie didn't have the most expensive dress, but it was an elegant one; Jennie helped her make it.

Annie's aunt hosted the wedding, near Auburn. Her aunt had invited a fiddle player, and it was a summer wedding, so they gathered in the farmyard. There was lemonade, coffee, and homemade cake. No alcohol was served, especially to a young couple like this. Everyone began clapping for Annie and Samuel to dance. Turns out, this was her first dance ever. She felt him lift her off the ground and whirl her around. What a wonderful day that was. So much of life now lay ahead of Annie . . .

CHAPTER 3

Life and Loss

From Auburn, Samuel and Annie moved to Bay City, Michigan. She was so excited for a fresh start. She felt sure that was what she needed: a fresh start with her own family. Samuel and Annie settled down in a tiny house, but to the two of them this small place was everything; it was their beginning together. To a family she wanted so badly to replace the family she had lost.

Samuel was always kind and gentle with her and would listen patiently to her dreams for both of them. He would hold her tight with his muscular arms and say, "Annie, I'm never letting go of you." Then he would laugh, and she would giggle over the same silly thing. They perceived this marriage was an adventure to be shared together; for them, it would not be a drudgery, as was so common for so many women and some men. He was her best friend, confidant, and lover all in one person. She knew no one could replace her Samuel. When he looked at her, he always had that twinkle in his eye; she was his girl. Annie smiled when she thought of him; she held on to the memories of Samuel as tightly as he held her in his arms. Their time together as husband and wife was the best of her life.

When she became pregnant, both were ecstatic. Finally the beginning, Annie told herself, the confirmation of their new family, of their blessed union together.

Annie had a difficult pregnancy, seemed always sick, her feet swollen, her face greasy—and oh, the nausea. Pregnancy was hard on her; even her doctor worried about her sickness. When their little son was born, he came early. He was tiny and had difficulty breathing, but he made it through the delivery to the care room.

She and Samuel hung on his every breath; sadly, he only lived a few days. They were both crushed as the tiny body of their son went, finally, limp and lifeless. He held their hearts in his little body, and his passing seemed unbearable for both her and Samuel. (There is no record of the son's name, if he was given one.)

Samuel did his best to show strength after his little son's death. He told Annie they would have many more babies to love. But it was all extremely hard on him as well.

CHAPTER 4

Heartbreak at Gettysburg

After the death of their child, Samuel became restless. He had a good, safe job working at the loading docks in Bay City. But his grief, at times, left him despondent. He thought maybe a break from Michigan would be best for both he and Annie. It would help put his life in a better perspective. Perhaps things wouldn't seem so bleak if they returned home to New York and family, Samuel reasoned.

Samuel and Annie were in so much pain they shut each other out. He went to work, she kept house, and when he got home they would eat in silence. Then Annie would read and Samuel would go outside for a smoke and relax. He didn't want to sell their home in Michigan. It was paid in full, but what had once been their cozy haven was now a place of depression and sadness. The rooms seemed empty; so were their hearts.

Samuel's plan was to move back home to Yates County, New York.[10] He felt bad about leaving Michigan, but hopefully, after they recovered from the loss of their child, they would move back, he told himself. Samuel felt he had somehow failed Annie when their son passed, but, of course, there wasn't anything he could have done to change the outcome.

> For her, it would be a new home, and once again a fresh start. Annie couldn't quite understand why Samuel found it so hard to let go of their first home.

For Annie's part, she found herself happy about moving back to New York. She viewed it as a chance to catch up with old friends and family. For her, it would be a new home, and once again a fresh start. Annie couldn't quite understand why Samuel found it so hard to let go of their first home. Although they had made some wonderful memories in Michigan, hopefully in their new home, back in New York, they would develop many more memorable experiences.

But, along with their move, came the War Between the States.

One of the reasons Samuel wanted to move back to New York was he believed it was his clear duty to enlist in the Union Army. His family had a history of war heroes, and he was not one to shy from conflict. The year was 1863, and the great war seemed to be reaching a crucial point. He was sure his participation could make a difference. One problem: he had not yet discussed his intention to enlist with Annie. He felt it best not to, at least not until they were settled in their new home. At the point they were committing to move, Samuel thought, the announcement of his going to war might be too much for her. At any rate, another important aspect of moving back was that, if anything happened, Annie would be close to family who could help her. He did make the decision to actually keep the little house in Bay City as it was paid for and close to his family.

They moved back to New York and settled in quite nicely. Annie's brother, Delano Edson, had married Samuel's sister, Jane—Annie's school roommate, Jennie. All of them soon became very close. Samuel and Delano felt the same about the great war: both felt called to do their duty for their country; both men believed their participation could make a difference. Both enlisted in the Army. It was June 1863.[11]

Samuel held Annie close when he finally told her he was going. He explained that most enlistments were only for three months, and he would be back home before she even missed him. In a way, he thought a short separation would be good for them. Perhaps both of them could work through their grief in their own way and they would come back together stronger.

> Perhaps both of them could work through their grief in their own way and they would come back together stronger.

Samuel was assigned a corporal's rank in his unit. He had been in his unit not even thirty days when it was ordered to head toward the small town of Gettysburg, in southeast Pennsylvania. The Confederate Army under General Robert E. Lee was headed that way. New York sent 23,050 of its finest men to stop the movement of the Confederate Army. The Union amassed about 78,000 in total in the great conflict, the Confederates about 15,000 less than that.

Dozens if not hundreds of books have detailed the three full days of battle at Gettysburg; it is not this book's intention to recast those events here. But the first key fact one can find about New York's engagement is this: the state lost 6,695 of its men in this bloodiest, most tragedy-filled battle of the Civil War.[12]

It was a hot, humid early July day. Samuel and the other men were tensely awaiting the signal from their captain to go into battle. There had been sporadic shooting, but nothing major yet. Samuel awaited the battle with his head held high, wanting to defend the Union. Suddenly, a bugle call, and he and the other men holding their rifles with bayonets charged the Confederate soldiers across an open field. The sounds of cannon balls whizzing through the air over their heads and gunshots barely missing them were not deterrents to their charge. As the battle progressed some soldiers who had run out of bullets were left to fight only with bayonets. Others who had lost their rifles were engaging in hand-to-hand combat. Soldiers were falling all around Samuel; the scene was chaotic and bloody.

This was some of the fiercest fighting. Samuel *heard*—as well as felt—a shot rip into his chest. He found the pain terrible but hung on. He continued fighting until his unit was down to its last men. He finally passed out from pain, loss of blood, and exhaustion.

After the battle was over, Union members searching the field found Samuel alive, barely, yet badly wounded. They rushed him to a makeshift hospital in Gettysburg; due to the battle the town was sadly lacking medical supplies, food, and water.

Samuel died three days later, on July 6, 1863.

There was a knock at the door. Probably one of her in-laws, Annie thought, as they had been kind to check on her frequently while Samuel was gone. Instead, it was their minister, his face white, a drained white, and he looked exhausted. He held his head down as if afraid to look at her. He asked Annie if he could come in and sit down; she nodded yes. By coincidence, he actually found a seat in Samuel's chair. He took her hand and started crying; he couldn't speak. Annie knew what was coming. He said, "Samuel fought to the very end in the Battle of Gettysburg. And he fought to stay alive. When they finally found him, they rushed him to the hospital, but it wasn't enough. He passed from his wounds on July 6th. I'm so sorry, Annie."

Annie went into shock. She couldn't speak, she couldn't think. This was not real; she was having a nightmare. She dropped the minister's hand, turned, and walked away, but then passed out.

The next three weeks were a blur.

Annie was often driven back to the thought that they had been married only seven years! She would shake her head. How could she survive this? She thought she was going to die herself. It was as if her heart had been broken in a thousand pieces. She couldn't think properly; it was like her heart and mind had been pulled out of her body and there was nothing left.

For those next three weeks she could hardly get out of bed. She did make it to the short funeral services, one for her husband and the other for her brother Delano.[13] A week after receiving the news of Samuel, she found out her dearest older brother also had died from wounds suffered in the battle. Delano passed on July 13, seven days after Samuel. Jennie, her sister-in-law, was inconsolable. Annie was numb and in a state of shock.

Samuel's family later became somewhat upset with Annie, saying she did not present the proper picture of a grieving widow. But how would they know her grief? She was grieving both Samuel and their son, the dear, sweet baby boy they had lost, the grief of which nearly killed them at the time. She would hold her head in her hands while trying to talk to them, just shaking her head. The memories of their baby boy still hurt, much like razors cutting into her soul.

In this era a woman was taught not to feel sorry for herself or show grief publicly. She was simply to move on with her life.

After the three weeks, Annie told herself she needed to move on. She couldn't think of the losses anymore. *Time to move forward and think about the tasks ahead,* she told herself sternly. No self-pity would be allowed. She had to be strong and move forward.

In this era a woman was taught not to feel sorry for herself or show grief publicly. She was simply to move on with her life. The common opinion was there was nothing worse than feeling sorry for yourself or asking for charity. And yet, Annie couldn't think of her losses without tears welling up. So, she told herself, it was better she didn't think of the past—at all—when in the public eye, and neither should she speak or write of it in any depth. She felt as though she had been through her own war. Her war, though, was the larger battle called life—and she felt she had no weapons to fight back.

CHAPTER 5

A Daredevil's Dream Barrel

1901. Annie told herself, *Think. Think! Is this going to work?* She had spent serious time designing this barrel, the barrel that would take her over Niagara Falls and, hopefully, into fame and fortune. But she had heard from numerous detractors and people analyzing her plan: "If the barrel doesn't hold together, her body will be dashed cruelly against the rocks below," they would say. "She could become an invalid, or worse."

But this is what they didn't understand: the thought of dying didn't bother Annie, because she would then be with her sweet Samuel and their son. Even though it had been nearly four decades since their passing, the memories still seemed so fresh. No, it was the thought of being an invalid and at the mercy of others that frightened her.

When she had conceived this idea, Annie "immediately set to work to shape a barrel, cutting it out of thick stock paper and sewing it together with twine. The dimensions: 22 inches at the head, 34 inches at the middle, and 15 inches at its foot. The barrel was 4 ½ feet high and weighed 160 pounds.

It was made of white Kentucky oak, with ten hoops, each riveted every four inches. The barrel was made by Bocenchia of West Bay City."[14] She shook her head. *Yes, this will work,* she thought to herself.

She also had placed two straps in the barrel, "a woven strap around my waist, and a strap from the back which went through the eye in the front of the barrel, fastened in front. This was to keep my head from violent contact with the barrel," she wrote.[15] Her hope was that these straps would hold her tightly in place and protect her from head and bodily injuries . . .

. . . Annie's mind wandered back to when she enrolled in Normal State School in Albany, New York, a school for teachers, some time after Samuel's death. As a widow, she was pretty much at the mercy of everyone, so she had to find a respectable way to support herself. She felt quite fortunate that the school accepted her— after all, she was an orphan, and then a widow—and her income was quite limited. Annie worked extremely hard to complete her degree. She felt this was her only chance to support herself with dignity and respect. There was a big demand for schoolteachers at the time, so her education was free.

Annie worked extremely hard to complete her degree. She felt this was her only chance to support herself with dignity and respect.

While attending the college she became good friends with two young ladies: Kate and Mary Kingsbury[16] from Texas. The sisters had been so impressed with Annie's seeming worldliness even though she was an orphan: a young married woman with a child, then having lost that child, then a war widow. The two sisters asked her to come stay with them for a year at their Texas home. . . .

. . . She broke her train of thought on Kate and Mary. She was getting nearer her Falls attempt. Annie stopped to look through her suitcase. She groaned; she was so limited in clothes. She only had one good outfit to present herself to the newspapers and public. A nice hat, street skirt, and coat. Underneath she would wear a comfortable shirtwaist and an informal skirt. She realized that before she went in the barrel she would have to take off her hat, street skirt, and coat, but she would have enough on underneath to not expose herself in any way. Through it all, she wanted to be sure to remain a respectable lady . . .

Annie thought back to the sisters, whom she called "Miss Kate and Miss Mary." What a year that was! After graduation she had been invited to spend a full year at their home.[17] She had been so thrilled and excited—a chance to travel and socialize with the upper class! Maybe a chance to advance herself socially. Kate had married Annie's cousin (socially, it was a big step up for her) and moved to San Antonio.[18] What grand plans Annie had for her life at that time—only to be disappointed over and over again . . .

> She had been so thrilled and excited—a chance to travel and socialize with the upper class! Maybe a chance to advance herself socially.

* * * * *

Now here she was in Buffalo, New York, on the verge of attempting a stunt that could kill her or . . . catapult her to fame. How had she come to this desperate last attempt at success? She had no money and only a few loyal friends. Her in-laws and most of her family had disowned her a long time ago. She was relying on an agent she had found in Bay City, Michigan, a Mr. F. M. Russell.

She prayed that this gentleman could help her.[19]

CHAPTER 6

From Cuba to San Antonio

Was it a mistake to travel to Texas? Annie turned this question over in her mind as she slipped on her stockings . . .

Ms. Kate and Ms. Mary Kingsbury had so wanted her to come see them they had paid her way, but Annie's family and friends very much objected to her going. She knew it was rather scandalous for a widow her age[20] to travel to Texas by herself, but she so loved the thought of a great adventure, and maybe she would find a new love there.

But then there was Cuba. On an impulse, she had decided to go, and was there for almost two months. What a time she had on that lovely island . . .

. . . Annie sat down at the desk chair, the only chair in her depressingly low-rent boarding house room, and took a deep breath. The Falls was just ahead of her, and yet her mind kept drifting back. If only she could have that time back . . .

What a wonderful, exciting, romantic time in her life it was—but it also seemed she had made so many wrong decisions. Annie was very intelligent; she had even taught herself Spanish before she attempted the trip. Oh how she loved Cuba, a tropical paradise with so many beautiful birds and flowers. It was so busy there, never boring, the bustling seaport of Havana, the music, the soft strings of the Spanish guitar, the romance and excitement in the air. So many travelers, seemingly all so friendly and helpful to her, especially the businessmen and even the gamblers, from the States like her, who were there for business—but adventure too. The weather was so fair; it always felt so good to step out of her hotel and onto the streets with the vendors and the women in their bright colorful dresses—all the colors of a rainbow. It was fascinating, everything she ever dreamed.

Except she was young and naïve. She winced as she thought about that. What a great fool she had been, thinking that someday things would work out—but they never had. Annie could only feel a bit sorry for herself . . .

Here I am getting ready to risk my life going over the Falls in a barrel, as a last resort. I have no income, nothing, a dried-up piece of land in Texas I can't sell. What is to become of me? . . .

Her thoughts went back to Calvin. Everyone called him Cal. She met him in Cuba. He was so handsome, tall and slender and about five years older

But this Calvin, Cal . . . he dazzled her, and best of all he told her he was single and traveling to Texas as well! He seemed so honest and sincere.

than Annie. He asked her to take an afternoon stroll so they could take in the sights and sounds of Cuba together. He was so gentle and strong, and exciting, much like her Samuel, who she had lost so young. She had been so desperately lonely for the companionship of a gentleman like the man she had married.

Yet she had not taken up with anyone since she lost her Samuel. But this Calvin, *Cal* . . . he dazzled her, and best of all he told her he was single and traveling to Texas as well! He seemed so honest and sincere; he spoke softly and with a wonderful southern accent. His eyes were crystal blue; he had thick, silky brownish-blond hair and a wonderfully stylish mustache and sideburns. He also had an extravagant style of dress, one Annie hadn't seen in New York in that period. He wore an expensive black suit with a beautiful ruffled white shirt and fancy brocaded vest. He had a gold chain across his vest and dazzling rings on each hand. Annie did not realize at first that this was typically the standard dress for professional gamblers. She had never seen a man so handsome, so flashy. She was terribly attracted to him, yet also somewhat wary of him, especially with his standard of dress.[21]

Before she knew it, her time to leave Cuba was near. She had been seeing Calvin almost a month and was scheduled to leave in a few days. Cal took her dancing; this was something she hadn't done since her wedding day! Afterward he invited her to his suite, which had a sitting room and an open balcony, where they could sit and look out at the city lights. The smell of the flowers and the warm night were intoxicating; the soft string music of a Spanish guitar wafted in the air. Cal offered her a glass of wine; it was so sweet and good. Before she knew it, he had leaned over and was kissing her. She could not stop him or push him away; she needed him too much. His kisses set her flesh on fire; she had denied herself of any feelings or longings for so long—since she lost her dearest Samuel.

Afterward Annie started crying, saying she had sinned, but she couldn't help herself. Cal asked her gently how long it had been since she had been with a man. Tears filled her eyes. She said it had not been since she was with her dearest Samuel. This took Cal back a little. He was used to the more hardened and jaded ladies out west; he thought maybe her story was not quite true, but then he realized she had told him the truth from the heart. He felt like he had just taken the innocence from an orphan; he was at a loss for words.

Calvin took a few minutes to make clear to Annie that he was a professional gambler. He had held off telling her, he said, since some women found that profession unacceptable. But in reality, in that day and age, gambling was considered an honest profession, especially out west.

It took Annie a while, but when she told him she was a widow and how young she had been widowed, and about the loss of their only child, Cal seemed shocked and concerned at the same time. He put his muscular arms around her and held her as she sobbed. He caressed her cheek and lovingly wiped her tears, listening intently to the story of her life and struggles after she lost her father and mother . . .

Before much longer, they were moving on. Cal traveled with her by ship from Cuba to Galveston, Texas. By this time people were talking; Annie told anyone who inquired that they were engaged. She was afraid of what they might say otherwise. Cal was OK with that; he liked the idea of people thinking he was engaged to such a beautiful and intelligent young woman. And he hoped to make this relationship official one day. In the meantime, he was just hoping that once they arrived in San Antonio, they would still be together. He knew, however, that he had better give this some time; he had been duped by women before.

Annie became a little seasick on the boat, but she loved the smell of the sea and the cool breezes that came up all at once. She found the sea mesmerizing, somewhat like a song one loves to hear over and over again.

Although she found her relationship with Cal troubling yet exciting (he was a professional *gambler*, after all), she could not contain her excitement over getting to see the great state of Texas and the growing city of Galveston, often referred to as "the New York of the Gulf," a bustling, growing port city, the "largest city in Texas."[22]

He wanted her so much, her petite but athletic figure, her big, sad eyes; those eyes had seen too much grief for one only in her early forties.

While in Galveston, Cal paid close attention to Annie, never letting her wander far from him. He wanted her so much, her petite but athletic figure, her big, sad eyes; those eyes had seen too much grief for one only in her early forties. He worried about her, traveling all alone from New York to Cuba, and then planning to do so while going on to Texas. Only a woman very brave—and probably a bit naïve, he figured— would have attempted such a trip without a proper companion. Although she had no one to watch over her—until him, that is—Cal realized this traveling on her own was through no fault of hers. Her siblings were busy raising families and working. She truly was an orphan—in every way.

Even though Cal had ventured out into the world at an early age—he was still in his teens when he left home—he felt protective and loving toward Annie. She was such a waifish and yet heroic figure to him, trying so hard to make her way in a world full of cruel, conniving people. Cal sighed. Was he one of those people? There are some moral dilemmas that are wrong, yet justifiable in one's natural mind; was he justifying this dalliance? He honestly did not know. All he knew was he wanted to protect her, and hopefully cement this relationship, before she arrived at her friends' home in San Antonio. So . . . what was Annie thinking traveling without a companion? Annie's school friends in San Antonio were sincere in helping her. Offering to have her come stay in their home for a year was a most kind and generous offer. He knew from talking to her that Annie was hoping to find her niche in San Antonio. Simply put, she had felt lost and at odds since the loss of her baby and husband. Her friends were anxiously awaiting her arrival and the chance to reminisce about the fun times they had at the Normal School in Albany. Cal felt these women surely were genuinely good people but were still basically schoolgirls as far as he was concerned, probably fascinated by Annie's supposed worldliness, she being an orphan and widow.

Annie loved Galveston. It was such a busy port city with a great diversity of people. She and Cal tried Italian food for the first time; both loved it. The spaghetti and meatballs were her favorite, Cal liked the lasagna, and the big thick loaf of hot Italian bread they were served was wonderful. She enjoyed her days in Galveston but knew she wouldn't be there long; it would soon be time to take the railroad to Austin.

Even though Kate and Mary had provided her passage to San Antonio, a gesture quite kind of them, Annie booked the cheap seats on the train. Cal upgraded her seat to first class so they could sit together on their way to Austin, the state capital. She couldn't wait to see it! She had read about it before her trip; she wanted to walk down Congress Avenue where all the state legislators and governor walked. And she wanted to see it at night when it was illuminated by gas lights.[23] She greatly wanted to ride one of the mule-driven streetcars. There was a lovely evening where she and Cal took a walk so they could see the "violet crown of Austin," a brilliant glow of violet color across the hills just after sunset.[24] It was such a nice evening, just cool enough to make a brisk walk comfortable. But beyond that, she greatly enjoyed the companionship of a gentleman who had come to mean the world to her.

> There was a lovely evening where she and Cal took a walk so they could see the "violet crown of Austin," a brilliant glow of violet color across the hills just after sunset.

Cal was excited too: a whole week together in Austin, and then they would be heading to San Antonio. In that growing Western city, he hoped to play for some real money. He and Annie stayed at a hotel in Austin (separate rooms, of course) that was near Congress Avenue. The hotel itself was nice for the times, but Austin was still part of the Wild West, and the hotels here were not like the luxurious hotels back East. Annie's room was basically a bed and a chamber pot.

Their time in Austin went too fast. Before they knew it, it was time to head to San Antonio. This would be one of the toughest legs of the trip. Although one of the shorter travel distances, it would be one of the more arduous trips.

Cal hated the idea of being separated from Annie even though they would both be in San Antonio at the same time. She would be staying with her friends and he would be staying at a hotel in another part of town. Also, Annie wasn't really anxious to share the news about her new beau with the Kingsbury sisters, and Cal understood this. Cal also knew he needed to keep a low profile because he had made a few enemies along the way.

They would take the stagecoach to San Antonio. Cal accompanied Annie to the station. The *Texas Almanac* has an entry in which an "old-timer" recounts what the trip was like:

"[It] was made in 18 hours with breakfast at the Blanco Creek, supper in New Braunfels, and arrival at San Antonio sometime during the night, weather and floods permitting. In wet weather, the 75-mile trip took the worst part of a week."[25]

Annie pulled her shoes on slowly while shaking her head. She was so close to her Falls attempt, and this was going through her mind: *When you are young and pretty, everyone wants to talk to you. But now I'm older, and not as attractive, nor as ignorant of the world's ways as when I was young. People, especially men, aren't as kind and friendly.*

As she moved slowly through her room, she thought back to that stagecoach ride, dusty and dirty as it was—not her cup of tea. But it was exciting, and she got to travel with Cal. Oh, how she loved Texas! But most of all, how much she loved Cal at that time. It was one of the best times of her life . . .

Annie and Cal had to be ready at the crack of dawn. The 75 miles to San Antonio were covered over uneven, dusty, rutty roads; it would be at least 18 hours for this trip. They would stop for breakfast at the town of Blanco Creek, which was a small settlement of farms and ranches near the actual Blanco Creek. The area was quite scenic, a wide creek that sprawled across the Texas range. Occasionally you would see a cabin or ranch house, maybe some cowboys riding the range herding cattle. Since the stagecoach line ran mail through this route, there was a small inn that served breakfast. The morning meal was basically whatever the inn owner had on hand at the time.[26]

With any luck they would be dining at the Schmitz Hotel in New Braunfels. The Schmitz was one of the finer places to stay. Built in the Classical Revival style, it stood out against the many saltbox-style homes. New Braunfels was a German settlement established by Prince Carl of Solms-Braunfels, Germany. The settlement was located along the Balcones Fault, where the Texas Hill Country meets rolling prairie land. Along the fault in the city, a string of artesian springs known as Comal Springs gives rise to the Comal River, which is known as one of the shortest rivers in the world; it winds three miles through the city before meeting the Guadalupe River.[27]

> She was thankful when she boarded that there were two nuns aboard heading for San Antonio and that she was with Cal.

Since this was a well-traveled route, Annie and Cal would be riding in one of the better coaches, a twelve-passenger Concord, bright red with yellow trim and pulled by a team of six horses. She was thankful when she boarded that there were two nuns aboard heading for San Antonio and that she was with Cal, as the rest of the passengers were men, and a couple of them looked rough to her. Ultimately, how they looked didn't make much difference, though; she had learned in her travels that the clothes generally *don't* define the man. She had had to fight off some very well-dressed men who did not act like gentlemen at all. Annie scooted up next to the nuns, as much for protection as company. Cal scooted in next to her and gave her an odd look. Her idea worked, however; when the other passengers saw her sitting with the nuns, they assumed she was traveling with them and pretty much left her alone. Cal, though, stood out like a sore thumb. The nuns were kind and made polite conversation with both of them.

The last man to take his seat on the coach did a double take as soon as he saw Cal with Annie and the nuns. He was a rough-looking man and smelled of alcohol and tobacco. He looked at Cal and shook his head. "My, my," the man said. "What is the likes of you doing with two nuns and this young lady?" Calvin was quick to answer. "I'm accompanying this young lady to the home of Misses Kate and Mary Kingsbury. I am responsible for her safety and well-being." The man just laughed. "Nothing like leaving the fox in charge of the henhouse," he grunted. Cal gave him a stern look, the man turned the other way, and from then on he left them alone. Annie had heard this fox-and-henhouse expression before, but she didn't understand how it would apply to her, Cal, and the nuns.

As they rode, Annie was left to ponder what this new adventure and her visit with Kate and Mary would bring. She hoped, perhaps, to procure a position with a good school in the growing and bustling city of San Antonio, to make Texas her home. She was also hoping she would get to spend much more time with Cal and possibly settle down with him there.

She was exhausted when they reached San Antonio, but thankfully Mary had sent a buggy for her. Small kindnesses:

sometimes those are the ones you appreciate most. To Annie's dismay, though, Cal wouldn't get in the buggy. He told her, "I have the address you gave me for Misses Kate and Mary. In a few days, when it's proper, I will come and call on you. You need a few days to unwind, and I have business to take care of. Please take good care of yourself, and I will see you in a couple of days."

Cal didn't kiss her goodbye. In truth, Annie was a little relieved Cal didn't take the final buggy. This was unfamiliar territory for her and she didn't know how her hostesses would react to the fact that she had a beau. She would deal with that situation, she told herself, when the time was right. She asked the driver if it would be OK to offer a ride to the nuns, and he nodded yes. Both gratefully accepted, and the driver took them to the convent first.

CHAPTER 7

San Antonio Blues

Annie looked around the dingy room. Hopefully, after today, she wouldn't have to stay in these sorts of places but could afford hotels which were a little more elegant and refined. She was depending on this stunt, and her manager, Frank M. Russell, to pull her out of debt and into a more profitable and comfortable lifestyle.

She sighed, and once again, her thoughts drifted back . . .

After Cuba, Galveston, and Austin, Annie's life in San Antonio changed—just not for the better. Kate and Mary helped her land a teaching position at a San Antonio high school as she had hoped, but life, with its twists and turns, had not worked out well for her there. She and Cal continued to see each other, but they also did their best to be discreet. Annie wasn't sure how her friends would feel about her being involved with a gambler. She didn't realize how notorious Cal actually was until she overheard Kate and Mary talking with some friends one day about the ills of gambling. They joked about losing their money to the likes of Cal, referring to him specifically.

Soon after Annie secured her teaching position, she rented her own room on Kingsbury Street. While she was teaching at the school she became friends with some of Mary's friends, officers and their wives. One month she traveled with a group of officers and their families on a vacation to New Mexico, where they journeyed into the mountains. An officer traveling with the party, a Captain Nolan, oversaw a detail of soldiers in the area. The soldiers were there to guard the construction of a new railroad through the mountains. Annie's group was traveling an overland route, but nonetheless they were in jeopardy of an attack from the indigenous tribes of the area.[28] Captain Nolan cut a handsome figure. He was brave and smart and knew how to fend off any enemy; Annie definitely admired him. She loved Texas and New Mexico, but her luck was about to run out in this corner of the world.

There were two incidents that took place out of her control, and they traumatized her. The first occurred while she was staying in her rooming house on Kingsbury Street. Part of her agreement was to take in the surrounding rents for the Kingsbury family, acting as their rental agent when they were out of town. One night, a thief broke in, chloroformed her, and stole three thousand dollars. From that point on, Annie didn't feel safe in the house.[29] She had trouble sleeping, tossing and turning at night, and this in turn caused her teaching skills to decline. It was a great deal of money to be stolen from her; the

> She had trouble sleeping, tossing and turning at night, and this in turn caused her teaching skills to decline.

Kingsburys had been kind and understanding about the situation and concerned for her well-being, but they were naturally upset over the money as well, and Annie felt terrible about the entire ordeal.

The second incident took place when she was riding a stagecoach from San Antonio back to Austin to begin her return trip home to New York. At one point, while the coach was traveling through a thick forest, bandits appeared out of the brush and ran down the transport. One robber pressed a gun to Annie's temple and demanded any money she might have. She couldn't believe her next words, but perhaps her desperation had reached its limit, and they came out of her all the same. "Blow away," she said as calmly as she could. "I would as soon be without brains as without money." This was a startling statement to the robbers and, realizing her desperation equaled theirs, they let her be. She was so relieved to be able to keep the eight hundred dollars she had tucked in her dress. It was all she had.

Oh . . . Annie held her head. *I can't keep reminiscing.* It was like her life was playing out before her eyes. *I have to get to the business at hand!* There was a knock at her door. "How are you doing in there?" It was Mr. Russell, her manager. "I'm doing fine" was Annie's simple answer. She didn't want to open the door; she was only partially dressed. "Have you had anything to eat?" Russell asked. "Just toast and some fruit," she said. "I don't want to eat too much; I don't want to take a chance on getting sick in the barrel when I'm going over the Falls."[31]

"OK," Russell said from the other side of the door, shaking his head. "See you in a couple of hours."

Russell shook his head again as he walked away. This woman was different. The last thing he would be worried about was getting sick in the barrel. This could be her last meal. She's concerned about getting sick in the barrel! They were both desperate, he and Annie. Russell was always hoping to latch onto a star, someone he could promote and use to bring in some money. He had a sinking feeling in his stomach about this gig. But then, he could be wrong; he had been wrong before. He did have to admire her courage. There is no way he would have signed on for such a stunt! Going over Niagara Falls in a barrel!

> He had a sinking feeling in his stomach about this gig. But then, he could be wrong; he had been wrong before. He did have to admire her courage.

As he headed back out of the boarding house for a while, Russell too was left with his thoughts. *Well, hopefully this old bird won't kill herself, but no one has ever survived going over the Falls.* (Two poor souls had previously gone over the Falls; one was an accident and the other a suicide attempt. Neither survived. In time, research shows, fifteen more people, from 1901 through 2017, would mimic Annie's attempt in going over the Falls. Seven died; nine of those who attempted the feat lived, including Annie.)

CHAPTER 8

Pan-American Expo

This was the time of the Pan-American Exposition of 1901. It was going on right now—here—in Buffalo, New York. The Exposition had been open since May 1 and was due to be closed November 2, so its time was winding down. The whole country was excited about the Expo. As an example, five young men rode all the way from Newark, Ohio on a single cycle, a "Quintette" five-seater, to the Expo, a trip of 315 miles.[32] The Exposition grounds spread across 342 acres and were located between Delaware Park Lake to the south, the New York Central railroad track to the north, Delaware Avenue to the east, and Elmwood Avenue on the west. Buffalo was filled with excitement, and that was part of what drew Annie to this place to perform this stunt.

One of the major features of the Expo was the use of electric lighting, which utilized hydroelectric power generated by the nearby Falls. Many of the Exposition buildings, including the prominent Electric Tower, were covered in light bulbs creating a beautiful and unprecedented sight. The Expo Midway was filled with entertainment and consisted of more than forty exhibits. Some of the main Midway attractions included the House Upside Down, Cleopatra's Temple, and the Foreign Villages.[33]

Annie was so hoping that President William McKinley, just into his second term, would be present when she made her attempt. Sadly, though, he had been the victim of an assassination attempt on September 6, just seven weeks earlier, while in a receiving line at the Exposition's Temple of Music. McKinley was shot twice by anarchist Leon Czolgosz. Tragically, the President died eight days later, September 14, from infection and gangrene that developed in the wounds.[34]

Today—Annie's day to go over the Falls—was October 24. She wanted to do the stunt just a little more than a week before the Expo would close. She thought timing was very important; she would finish the Expo with an exciting stunt! The second main reason she had chosen this date: her birthday. . . .

. . . Annie again drifted back, thinking of Cal. How, when she left San Antonio, she flittered around like a butterfly for a few years looking for her niche—yet always keeping in touch with Cal. At that point in her life, she found herself counting the days until she could see him again . . .

CHAPTER 9

Putting on Dancing Shoes

Annie decided she would go to New York City for a year to take instruction in dance and physical culture under some of the best instructors in the country. What a challenge that was! She really enjoyed working with her instructors. The workouts were many, the days went by fast, and there was never enough sleep—but when she did sleep, she slept hard. Most nights she was totally exhausted. She was, however, in the best physical shape of her life.

It was the Gilded Age in New York City, the 1880s, one of the most exciting places on Earth! Businesses were booming, Broadway plays had just come into existence, the old rich and the new rich were commingling (to some extent)—everyone seemed to be flaunting wealth. There was the beautiful architecture of the buildings: the Gothic architecture of the American Museum of Natural History (completed in 1877) and the Metropolitan Museum of Art (1878).[35]

Then there were the sybaritic mansions of the old and newly rich, on Fifth Avenue, such as the one designed by Detlef

Lienau, who is credited with "introducing the mansard roof to New York; it was the crowning feature of his first large house (1850-1852) built at the southwest corner of Fifth Avenue and Tenth Street for a French merchant and banker." Lienau frequently mixed ideas from France and Germany and was a prominent architect during that era.[36] There were the famous hotels along Broadway, one of them the Hoffman House, which, along with being a luxurious hotel, had one of the most famous bars in New York City. It was known for its famous painting "Nymphs and Satyr," which was covered with a thick velvet drape—the men would find a way to peek at the painting through a mirror located adjacent to it. The bar had an all-male clientele; women were allowed in just once a week. This was truly the Victorian age. The Hoffman House, along with the Albemarle Hotel, took up key frontage along Broadway.[37]

> Hearing the stories of the extravagantly lush balls given by such families as the Astors and Vanderbilts greatly stirred Annie's imagination, even giving way to some colorful daydreams.

Hearing the stories of the extravagantly lush balls given by such families as the Astors and Vanderbilts greatly stirred Annie's imagination, even giving way to some colorful daydreams. But the fact was these families, known as New York's Elite 400, only grudgingly acknowledged, but refused to accept, the newly rich. Someone like Annie? Well, there was no way she would ever fit in that society.[38]

She found New York City fascinating in its contrasts. Annie would spend time watching the hordes of workers, including many newly arrived immigrants, chattering in their native tongues. She would partake in some of the delightful smorgasbord of eateries and restaurants offering many types of food. The experience of all kinds of humanity mixed in one place—it was a beautiful, diverse culture. And yet, at the same time, it was sad knowing that so many faced numerous challenges and hardships. The metropolis was different than any place she had ever seen. The women were so cosmopolitan in their choice of clothing—well, at least the rich ones. Their outfits were colorful and pristine, in tune with the time.

New York City during this period, unlike so many places in the United States, had virtually no middle class. A person was either super rich or poor, and there wasn't a lot of compassion for the poor. The poor lived mostly in tenements, many families in one or two rooms. If they were lucky, they might get an entire flat.[39]

This was the New York City that Annie traveled to with the goal of studying dance for a year. After spending her tumultuous year in San Antonio, New York City was as opposite an existence as one could imagine. Now officially her suitor, Calvin had much business to take care of, he said, business out west that a woman shouldn't be part of. When she told him she had always dreamed of taking dance classes in New York City, Cal immediately offered to put up the money. The situation in San Antonio had soured for both of them, and it was time to move on.

> After spending her tumultuous year in San Antonio, New York City was as opposite an existence as one could imagine.

Although Cal loved Annie more than he thought he could love anyone, he knew there was no place for her where he was headed—California's gold mining towns. Most of these towns were squalid and dirty, shacks in the middle of mudholes. The little towns popped up overnight and usually revolved around a saloon and a few brothels. There was no law in these towns; it was mostly gold miners and gamblers like Cal, men who were afraid of nothing and would risk everything for a few nuggets of gold. This was no place for Annie, Cal knew.

Although Cal loved Annie more than he thought he could love anyone, he knew there was no place for her where he was headed— California's gold mining towns.

He reasoned that if Annie could take dance instruction classes for a year, he could make good money in California gambling, maybe buy a place in Texas, and they could marry and settle down back in the Lone Star State. Annie had the same dream Cal did, but not quite the same optimism. She thought that perhaps with dance instruction she could help her reality as a poor widow and maybe acquire a position at one of the more elite dance academies in Texas or somewhere else in the country. She wanted things to work out for her and Cal. She even thought about seeking a part in one of the popular musicals or plays such as "The Pirates of Penzance," which opened in February 1882 at Booth's Theater, or the "The Royal Middy" at the Bijou Opera House. If she could land such a role, she knew, it would help pay her way since New York City was so very expensive.[40]

The New York City dance school where Cal helped bankroll her lessons was not as she imagined. She was thinking of one of the beautiful, classic buildings along Broadway or Fifth; this dance studio was in one of the poorer neighborhoods near the tenements. Wanting to be thrifty with her money, Annie rented a one-room flat where she shared a bath with five other roomers. What she paid for her flat in New York City she could have used to rent a whole house in San Antonio! But at least she avoided the tenements; that area was far too rough for a single widow by herself. She would be raped or murdered in her bed if she rented a room there, she was sure, and the conditions of the tenements were about as miserable as one could imagine. Fortunately, Annie found a flat within walking distance of the dance studio, and she passed a small grocer on her way to and from class. Most of her dinners consisted of bread, salted meat or cheese, and dried fruit; a piece of fresh fruit was a treat. A hot meal was a pleasure she allowed herself once or twice a week. She had to buy that meal at a small eatery; she had no way of cooking a nice meal or keeping food in her little flat. She washed her clothes in a bucket and hung them to dry in her room. In short, this was not the luxurious existence she had hoped for.

Her dance instructors were very good, very disciplined. They were a married couple who had emigrated from Europe; both had studied at the more well-known dance academies on the old continent. They were familiar with both dance and physical culture. Ellen was petite and yet stout like Annie. She was determined to make the school a success even though the academy was off to a meager start. Ellen's husband, Henry, was tall and thin but extremely muscular and had a wonderful sense of humor and the most reassuring way about him. Watching Ellen and Henry dance together was one of the most beautiful things Annie ever encountered. Their litheness and agility, their flowing together like a stream until they nearly became one on the dance floor . . . their movements accenting the other. It was simply inspiring.

They also taught physical culture classes, and these were helpful to Annie as well (she was invited to take part in a few), but they mainly targeted these classes for New York's upper class. Because of the economic structure at the time, only the upper crust could afford such classes on a regular basis. Most men of lesser means had jobs in hard labor, including toiling as steelworkers, factory workers, or railroad workers; all such occupations required a great deal of strength and prowess. Women of lesser means had chores around the house that were physically taxing; most women laundered their clothes in a bucket with a washboard by soaping the clothes and then scrubbing them vigorously against the board. They cleaned floors with a broom and rags or a mop, or on their hands and knees with a scrub brush. Children were expected to contribute either by helping around the house, running errands, or working at a very young age. Most people of lesser means walked to and from work or took the trolley; a horse and buggy were too expensive for the common worker in New York City.

Annie arrived at class every morning promptly at 8:45; class started at 9:00 a.m. sharp. Ellen and Henry were emphatic about the importance of promptness to their classes. When they started class, they wanted everyone on the same page, bright-eyed and fully ready to go. Ellen and Henry did not like repeating themselves; they expected their students to be good listeners and to diligently practice their dance moves in their free time so they would be sharp in class. Annie liked the few physical culture classes she could take part in, but she clearly enjoyed the dance classes most. When she was dancing it took her away from her troubles, her grief; all the losses didn't hurt as much when she was dancing. Sometimes Annie felt as if she was running from her grief and loneliness. She missed Cal so much.

One day, she received an invitation she did not expect.

"Annie," Ellen inquired, "would you like to have dinner with Henry and I tonight?" Annie was thrilled, if a bit stunned, to be invited to dine with her instructors.

"Yes, yes. I would like to dine with you . . . both," she stammered. "Thank you for the lovely invitation!"

Ellen and Henry lived directly above the studio. Their flat was not lavish, but it was warm and cozy and had a European feel. Dinner wasn't the most expensive food, but this hot, homemade meal was delicious! It was so nice to eat at a table set with fine china and silver on a crisp linen tablecloth. It was quite the contrast to the impoverished neighborhood Annie lived in and a welcome break from eating out of a paper bag nearly every night. They even had a teapot; hot tea was served with dessert. What a treat!

As dinner was beginning, Ellen started the conversation. "Annie, we invited you here tonight because Henry and I like to get to know our students. What was your life like before you came here?" She paused. "Also, you are an excellent student, and we wanted to congratulate you on that." Annie blushed just a bit. Ellen went on, circling back to her question. "What brings a young woman such as yourself to our dance school?"

Annie looked down. "I do have family—well, actually, one older brother, one sister, and three younger brothers. I am close with my sister, but they're all struggling and raising their families. If push came to shove I could ask them for help, but I do not wish to be a burden on anyone, and want to be able to support myself." Annie rocked back and forth while folding her arms in front of her as if to keep away the coldness of death. She paused, then went on. "My husband and I lost our beloved son, just a baby, when I was 20. Then in early July 1863 my husband was shot and killed in the Battle of Gettysburg. Also, my older brother died from wounds received in that battle. He died about a week after my Samuel."

Annie paused again. She didn't want to give the impression of self-pity. "I went to the Normal State School in Albany and graduated with honors to become a teacher. I love dance and physical culture and feel driven to teach. I am engaged to a very kind, understanding gentleman, but we agreed not to marry until we are financially set. So I need a proper way to support myself until then." Ellen stood, wiped away a few tears, and walked over to hug Annie. Softly, she said, "We are so sorry for your losses." Then she brightened. "We understand your drive to teach in the arts. Henry and I have dedicated ourselves to that as well." Henry patted Annie reassuringly on her hand across the table.

Ellen went on. "It's good to have a student who is not only dedicated but loves the arts as we do." Henry nodded and finally offered some words himself. "Yes, we will help you any way we can," he said.

These were two of the kindest people Annie had ever met. Many women became distant, even hostile, when they found out Annie was a widow. At the least, most were unsympathetic. Ellen and Henry, though, were not like that. Annie valued their friendship greatly and loved them like family.

Annie worked extremely hard that year to learn all she could. She knew this might be her only chance at this kind of education. Ellen and Henry, knowing how alone Annie was, tried to have her for dinner at least once a week. They sometimes wondered about her fiancé, but they didn't delve too deeply, not wanting to offend her. For her part, Annie didn't want to do anything to undermine their friendship. So she couldn't bring herself to tell them about Cal, that he was not actually her fiancé yet, but that she was waiting until he was ready to settle down.

The year seemed to go too fast. It was hard to say goodbye to Ellen and Henry when the year's classes came to a close.

Happily, though, she secured a position in Chattanooga, Tennessee—or thought she had.

When she arrived in Chattanooga, everything went sour.

CHAPTER 10

Burned Out in Chattanooga

Annie looked briefly out her hotel window. The Falls . . . this day . . . it all laid ahead of her. Pensively, she allowed herself to think back to Chattanooga. There was no other way to view it: Chattanooga was a terrible experience . . .

. . . She had thought her stay in the southeast Tennessee city would be a pleasant experience because, at the time, it was booming with new industry and opportunity. Calvin had recommended Chattanooga to her until they could meet up again. Calvin was a southern-born gentleman and thus felt far more comfortable with Annie residing in the old South.

Annie stayed in a rooming house; there was no need for a whole house to herself. Her rent included a maid cleaning her room and providing her clean sheets once a week; she also received breakfast in the morning and a hot supper at night. Thus, she didn't have to worry with household chores other than rinsing out her personal garments. She found herself extremely tired after teaching physical culture and dancing all day. Mrs. Broom was the owner of the boarding house. It was easy to tell when she was having a good week—the meals were delicious—but when she was having a bad week, the meals weren't so good. Annie also knew not to upset Mrs. Broom by complaining, because sometimes the owner doled out the food, and if you were a complainer, you would get the coldest, hardest piece of meat—and were lucky to receive just half a portion of everything else.

Annie was hoping to settle in Chattanooga for a while. She told herself how much she would enjoy the mild weather here after a year in New York City. The people in this southern city were friendly enough, but the salary she received as a teacher was barely enough to live on. Annie had managed to save some money, and she hoped to invest it and create a nice little nest egg. Calvin had given her some money to invest for them as well. Annie met some folks in her neighborhood who were excited about the possibility of new industries starting up in Chattanooga.

One gentleman who befriended her was trying to establish his own business. Harry was most helpful to Annie when she first moved to the city; he had shown her around. He became a close friend and confidant. Annie was not attracted to him in any way, which was good since she was an completely committed to Cal, but she did find his friendship and confidence in her quite comforting. Annie could call for him anytime and he would be over to help fix whatever problem there might be. Harry was having trouble finding backers for his new business, a furniture factory and retail store, but finally found a couple of big-name bankers who said they would invest in his business if he could find two more investors. The names of the bankers were familiar to nearly everyone in the city, practically household names in Chattanooga. And so it was that Harry, looking for two more investors, turned to Annie.

If these gentlemen bankers had the confidence to invest in Harry, why shouldn't she? Why miss out on an opportunity of a lifetime, Annie asked herself. Now was the time, he assured her, to jump on the bandwagon. She remembered Harry saying, "Annie, you have a big heart. If only all should have a heart like you." When she made the decision that she would be the third investor, it took a big part of her and Cal's savings, about $1,700, which was a substantial amount. Harry was elated, Annie felt good about the investment, and she felt good about herself; it felt so beneficial to help a friend and invest in the future of a city. Annie felt so positive about the investment that she even wrote a long letter to Calvin explaining the venture. She was certain he would be pleased.

> If these gentlemen bankers had the confidence to invest in Harry, why shouldn't she? Why miss out on an opportunity of a lifetime, Annie asked herself.

After Annie placed her investment with Harry, she was, naturally, full of questions about the business. When would it be open for business? How many workers would Harry hire? As a full-fledged business investor, would he have a substantial place for her in the business?

After providing Harry the loan, suddenly the businessman wasn't as easy to reach on a daily or even weekly basis. He excused himself with "working on getting this business afoot" or "interviewing workers today." Annie decided to be direct. One day when she was able to meet with him, she asked, "When will there be a position for me? I'm thinking of working as one of the managers." Harry, startled, said "a lady such as yourself would never be employed in a factory. Down here, this is men's work." Earlier, she had considered opening her own dance school with her savings but hadn't been quite sure how to go about it, and Harry had made the furniture factory and store sound like such a wonderful deal.

Now heavy doubts were starting to seep in. "Well, I'll leave him alone for a couple of weeks," Annie told herself. "Then maybe he'll be more patient and take me and show me the factory." After three weeks of not hearing a word from Harry or how the business was going, she sent him a note saying she wished to speak with him. She heard nothing in return. Finally, Annie inquired with a mutual friend, Al, who also had made the leap to be an investor in the business. Al was the kind of man you could trust. He and his wife, Pam, were kind and friendly people. He was an older man, and his main concern was creating a strong nest egg for his wife Pam in case he became sick.

"What's going on here, Al?" Annie asked him that day. "I can't get ahold of Harry, and I haven't heard a word about town concerning his new business or what's going on." Al was heartsick that day to tell Annie what he knew. If he could have reached Harry he would have tarred and feathered him and had him carried out of Chattanooga on a railroad tie.

"I'm sorry, Annie. I truly am. I thought Harry was the real deal." He took a breath. "He absconded with all the money from the investors in the middle of the night. He stuck around long enough to make folks like us think he was truly working on this project. But the truth be known, he had no intention of setting up a business. He was just biding his time until he could make a clean getaway." Annie gasped; she felt like some-

Annie gasped; she felt like someone had punched her in the stomach. This was most of her life's savings! This was her and Calvin's money to help them get a fresh start. She felt faint. Al grabbed her arm to help hold her up. She wanted to cry but didn't want to seem weak. Al felt so bad for her.

"Annie, we've taken this matter up with the sheriff," Al said. "If Harry does dare show his face in this town he will immediately be arrested. It's not just us he cheated but the bankers too. They are going to put out an award for information leading to his arrest." He paused. "Are you OK?" Annie nodded yes, but she wasn't. She just wanted to lay down and cry. What would she do now? She still had some money in her savings, but this made a huge dent in her finances, and Calvin would be so angry with her; he would also see her as a real dupe.

"Why don't you come spend the evening with Pam and I?" Al offered. "We will fix you a nice dinner and talk about this. Maybe there is some way we could retrieve your money, at least." Annie nodded that she appreciated the offer. She couldn't give up hope; she knew that would be the worst thing she could do.

Al, Pam, and Annie had an enjoyable dinner, talked, and laughed, but had an observer been in the house that evening they would have been able to tell by their faces that all three were hurting. Al and Pam were trusting souls and had thought the world of Harry. They had been greatly wounded by the situation. They were not rich, just careful with their money, and they had been looking for a promising business to wisely invest in. By the end of an otherwise fine evening all three had come to the realization that there was not a lot they could do to recover their money. Al and Pam took Annie home in their carriage. It was a long, silent ride, an unspoken heaviness hanging in the air.

It had been less than a week since Al delivered the bad news. The only good thing about the week was the wonderful dinners that Mrs. Broom, the boarding house owner, served. Usually, she offered a lot of fried bologna, but not this week. Mrs. Broom was a widow, and a handsome, middle-aged boarder had just rented one of her rooms. The dinners since this man arrived were outstanding: southern fried chicken, catfish, or country fried steak, and always homemade bread or biscuits with jam. The new boarder, Mr. Wiggins, was an interesting man; he liked to smoke cigars, and he also drank a little too much at times, falling asleep with a cigar in his mouth.

When Annie opened the door, the doorknob hit Wiggins directly in the eye! Annie squealed, and Wiggins took off for his room.

Annie had one bad run-in with Wiggins. Having stayed in boarding houses before, she knew there was usually a peephole in the bathroom, or sometimes, if not a peephole, a large keyhole; this boarding house had a large keyhole. Annie always tried to remember to take her handkerchief and stuff it in the keyhole. One evening she forgot her handkerchief; she was very tired and had had an exhausting day teaching dance and physical culture. Also, she remained heavyhearted about the loss of her money. She just wanted to take a quick "bath" from her marble sink and go to bed. When Annie opened the door, the doorknob hit Wiggins directly in the eye! Annie squealed, and Wiggins took off for his room. Mrs. Broom peered out her door to see what all the commotion was about.

The next night, at supper, Wiggins was extremely self-conscious about his black eye. When asked about it by one of the other boarders, he said he had gotten into a fistfight over a lady's honor. "But you should see the other guy!" he crowed. Mrs. Broom grimaced when he said that but kept her silence. She decided to dole out the food that night; she had a large skillet of southern fried chicken. As usual, Mr. Wiggins got the breast, and he smiled hugely at Mrs. Broom and winked when she put it on his plate. When she got to Annie, she took the smallest, hardest piece of chicken she could find and dropped it on her plate. Annie just ate it and didn't complain. *That's just the way these crazy old women are,* she told herself, quickly losing all faith in what she thought had been the fine city of Chattanooga.

A few nights later, things hit bottom. Someone was banging frantically at her door. The house was on fire! Annie ran to the street and saw other boarders with blankets around them, shocked looks on their faces. Wiggins was there too, his dark, curly hair singed and his hand showing a bad burn.

The house burned completely, to the ground, and no cause was ever found, or so it was said. Poor Mrs. Broom had to move in with her sister. The rest of them, the boarders, were on their own. Devastated, Annie had lost all her belongings, which were meager to begin with. The few items that really mattered to her were the keepsakes from her husband and son (her wedding dress, a baby blanket, and booties), a history book given to her by her father, and slippers from her mother. These were gone, along with all her other items, and no one but her would understand the special meaning of the keepsakes. Annie was done with Chattanooga. Her whole experience here had been something close to a nightmare.

But as they seemed to do, things kept evolving in Annie's life. She had been offered a position in Asheville, North Carolina. She told herself it was time to go!

> Annie was done with Chattanooga. Her whole experience here had been something close to a nightmare.

CHAPTER 11

Renewal in Asheville

Asheville was (and is) a beautiful town, bordered by the gorgeous Blue Ridge Mountains. Just ten thousand people resided there in 1886, and Annie was very much looking forward to this new location. She would be able to ride the entire distance by rail thanks to the East Tennessee, Virginia, and Georgia Railway system, and she was grateful for that; she had had quite enough of stagecoaches—and more than enough of Chattanooga!

Annie secured a temporary stay at the Swannanoa Hotel. She was to be a dance and physical culture teacher there for guests and their families; her employment included room and board. She was so excited; hopefully she could call this place home for a little while, at least through the tourist season. Then, after the summer was over, she would be headed to Washington, D.C. An old friend had contacted her through the mail asking if she could teach at a Young Ladies School for the winter season while her friend took an extended leave of absence.

The Swannanoa was a popular resort; people came there from all over the country. One source wrote: "Even in daytime a dance is going on in the Swannanoa ballroom on a level with the street. The strains of music from it and whirling figures seen from the sidewalk will be enough to clinch the opinion that you are in a gay and fashionable summer resort. Every week-day night dances are held at both the Swannanoa and Eagle [hotels]."[41]

By this time, though, Annie felt a bit jaded; she knew not to expect everything to be wonderful. Arriving in Asheville, she was met at the station by a buggy from the Swannanoa, and that was nice. The driver was extremely friendly and welcomed her to the hotel. She arrived and checked in with the general manager, who introduced himself as Don. He showed her to her room. It was small but comfy and had all the modern conveniences—electricity and a small bath with a tiny bathtub! That was fine with her after sharing a bath with five people at her New York City flat, and after one bath for all the boarders at Mrs. Broom's house (including its large keyhole)! What a luxury to be able to bathe as long as she wanted without someone banging at the door or having to hang a washrag over a peephole or stuffing the keyhole with a handkerchief.

> What a luxury to be able to bathe as long as she wanted without someone banging at the door or having to hang a washrag over a peephole or stuffing the keyhole with a handkerchief.

At the school, Annie was not the main teacher; the teacher in charge had classes in the morning and afternoon or upon request. It didn't matter if there were one or one hundred students; Annie was to be available to teach the guests to dance or in a class on physical culture. Her boss, Ms. Amanda, was very friendly, but she was older and seemed somewhat worldly to Annie. (Annie had thought herself fairly worldly for a woman her age.) Ms. Amanda took all her dance instructor women under her wing; she knew that most who ended up with her had faced a rough row to hoe and many, like Annie, were orphans or widows.

When Annie sat for her entrance interview, Ms. Amanda was quite impressed with her overall presentation; Annie was very clean and accounted well for herself. When Annie spoke, she spoke clearly, as one who had a higher education than her station in life indicated. Ms. Amanda even sought to put her at ease at one point, saying, "Relax, honey. You don't have to impress me. I know you're just here for the summer and that you have another engagement in Washington, D.C. for the winter when you are done here." Annie gratefully accepted some offered lemonade. Her mouth was dry, and she hated these interviews even though, for the most part, people were welcoming. Ms. Amanda, though, was someone she felt at ease with immediately. She seemed down to earth and, like Annie, probably had seen her share of tragedy.

Ms. Amanda looked at her directly, sizing her up. "May I ask why a beautiful, educated woman such as yourself is not married or settled into a permanent teaching position somewhere?" Annie looked down. Things should have gone better in San Antonio or Chattanooga, she told herself—but what was, was, and there was no sense looking back. It was too hard to explain everything to strangers, why she was down on her luck. She just whispered, with tears in her eyes, "I'm an orphan. I was orphaned at 14. I am also a widow. Our only son passed away a few days after he was born, and my husband was killed at the Battle of Gettysburg in Pennsylvania during the War between the States a few years after that." She paused. "I guess I'm still trying to find my way." There. At least she had been brutally honest. Ms. Amanda was taken back by Annie's confession. She knew her employee was being as honest as she could, and she also knew other things, bad things, had happened to Annie.

She didn't know exactly what to say, but she knew she didn't want to go much deeper with Annie. Ms. Amanda stammered, "I'm sorry. I didn't mean to pry into your life." After another pause came a question Annie didn't expect. "Do you smoke? Would you like a cigar?" She pulled out a small box of slender cigars; they had a wonderful aroma to them. Annie slowly reached to accept one. "No, I don't smoke. But I've always been curious, so yes, I would like to try one of these." Annie's first attempt at smoking: *Aaah!* It choked her, she gagged, made a face, and put the cigar down. Ms. Amanda was concerned but also slightly amused. Gently, she offered, "Here, just puff on it, and you will be OK." Annie took a drink of her lemonade, then tried the cigar again. "It's not bad," she said. "Actually relaxing—sort of."

"You don't want to overdo these, but occasionally a good cigar is nice," Ms. Amanda said with a smile. Annie nodded.

The dance teacher looked once more at Annie. "I'm a widow, first husband. Divorcee, second husband. So I'm a bit of a scandal around here, and I have, shall we say, male friends. Don't judge me, and I won't judge you. Also, there is no gossiping about guests, me, or other employees. That just stirs up trouble and loses customers. Be on time to all dance classes

Annie nodded dutifully. She was sick of gossips, and she was very serious about her teaching. It was also a bit of a relief, actually, to hear that Amanda had male friends and wasn't looking to judge her or anyone.

and all physical culture classes. Even if there is only one student, we give it our all. Each guest is important." Annie nodded dutifully. She was sick of gossips, and she was very serious about her teaching. It was also a bit of a relief, actually, to hear that Amanda had male friends and wasn't looking to judge her or anyone. Annie was hoping Calvin could join her here for at least a few days, just him and her.

Between her time here and going to Washington, D.C., it was a relief for Annie to know she wouldn't have to worry about Ms. Amanda judging her. Annie had smiled after Ms. Amanda made that statement, the non-judging one, and they talked and joked a bit. Annie felt she would enjoy a fine summer in this town.

And she did. She loved teaching dance in the ballroom. Most of those taking classes were tourists, and they weren't at all demanding; they just wished for a little instruction so they wouldn't look foolish on the dance floor later. Also, if she took a little extra time to instruct her students, they usually were most appreciative and gave her a pretty good tip. A lot of their appreciation was due to the fact Annie was a step above as a dance teacher, and most of her students realized she was the real deal, not someone just trying to make a few dollars for the summer. As Annie's expertise became known she grew to be in great demand as an instructor, and this meant she stayed very busy throughout that summer. She still had time, though, to take walks in the evening, and sometimes she would find a comfortable place to just sit and read after a long day of instruction. Annie enjoyed the laid-back atmosphere at the Swannanoa; everyone was kind to her, and no one judged her or gossiped about her. She greatly enjoyed the privacy she had in her room; it too was a refuge after a long day.

The summer went by quickly, but after she received a letter from Cal saying he was coming to Asheville to spend some time with her before she went to Washington, D.C., the days couldn't go by fast enough.

On a lovely late summer evening, Annie and Calvin were walking along the sidewalk next to Battery Park enjoying the view of the surrounding Blue Ridge Mountains. The mountains were so beautiful as they reflected purple and gold in the sunset. She would be leaving in a few days for a holiday with Cal down in Charleston, South Carolina, before then heading to Washington for another temporary appointment, this one for the winter, again teaching dance and physical culture.

The summer had gone by quite fast. She made many friends with other employees and guests. Ms. Amanda had told her she was welcome back anytime, which felt good, and Amanda did not seem surprised when Annie mentioned her fiancé was coming to see her before leaving for Washington. Amanda did seem to express a bit of surprise when she found what Annie's fiancé did for a living.

When Cal came to pick her up, he looked every bit as handsome and colorful as he did when Annie first met him in Cuba. His gambling must have been paying off as he sported a new black suit, brocade vest, and now a big ruby pin in front. Ms. Amanda's mouth dropped when Annie introduced them.

She said, "I've heard of you, but thought you were a legend." Cal was quick with an answer. "That's flattering, Ms. Amanda, to hear I'm so highly thought of. I appreciate the many kindnesses you've shown my Miss Annie."

Amanda pondered this scenario, and in her mind she came up with this: it was somewhat like seeing Little Red Riding Hood with the Big Bad Wolf. Although, at the same time, judging by the way Cal looked at her and treated her, Annie was truly the apple of his eye. Anyone who dared to hurt her would have him to deal with, and that would not be pleasant. In fact, Amanda had heard a story—she wasn't entirely sure if it was true or not—about some fellow in Chattanooga who had cheated a friend of Cal's out of money. Amanda wondered: *was this Annie?* The fellow ended up tarred and feathered, but they never found the money. (Lucky for the scoundrel, the law was looking for him too. He was probably lucky he was apprehended by marshals. He easily could have ended up in the bottom of some swamp had he not been sent off to prison.) Ms. Amanda studied Annie's face. Amanda could tell Annie was totally in love with Calvin and could see no bad in him. Amanda knew Annie had been faithful to Calvin through the entire summer. (Even though Amanda didn't want her employees gossiping, she did have a couple of close friends who kept an eye on things to keep down any trouble.)

Annie felt it was so good to see Cal again, but he seemed somewhat distracted. Cal was truly happy to see Annie, but he also knew he would have to do some extensive traveling to keep his gambling career profitable. That troubled him as he was simply hoping to spend more time with her.

The next morning, after a wonderful breakfast, they decided to take a walk. Cal was enjoying the stroll; he looked down at Annie, who was just chattering away telling him about her summer in Asheville and how much she liked it here. He looked on her with love and affection. He felt so protective of her. He was glad she had so enjoyed her time here; he just wished he could spend more time with her. But it was a beautiful day, and they were making the most of it, including a picnic in Battery Park—good bread, cheese, and wine. Simple, but enough to make them exceedingly happy. Later, they strolled at sunset in this beautiful place, and it felt almost ethereal to Annie. Life was absolutely perfect for a day.

In the morning both would be on the train to Charleston to spend a few days together at the Charleston Hotel before Annie headed to Washington and Cal back out West. It was August 29, 1886, and they were going to stay in Charleston through September 3. Calvin wanted to stay longer, but he also knew he was in a current run of good luck, and he didn't want to jinx things.

He had been able to bankroll some savings. He was still hoping he and Annie could buy that ranch in Texas and get married.

CHAPTER 12

An Historic Earthquake

Annie was so excited; she was greatly looking forward to this trip to Charleston, although it was not the resort spot Asheville was. Charleston is located next to Charleston Harbor, an inlet of the Atlantic Ocean formed by the confluence of the Ashley and Cooper rivers.[42] Charleston is the oldest city in South Carolina, a beautiful, historic city, one with "well-preserved architecture, distinguished restaurants, and mannerly people."[43]

It was a beautiful South Carolina evening, August 31, 1886. It was their third day there, and Annie and Cal had spent the morning walking and looking at the historic buildings in the city. For lunch they had packed a picnic and walked down to Charleston Harbor. It was so picturesque, watching the ocean and enjoying the beautiful weather. Cal surprised Annie by taking her to dinner at a very distinguished restaurant, one with white tablecloths, only the best china, and fresh flowers at each table. The waiter bowed when he introduced himself. Annie often felt as if she was part of the upper crust when she was with Calvin. But she also often had a nagging, troubling feeling, one of worry about his well-being since she knew his line of work could be risky if he met the wrong people.

Annie and Cal took their time with this exquisite, leisurely meal, which had five courses; she didn't think she had ever eaten this much in one sitting. The waiter ended the meal with dessert. Cal ordered a scrumptious-looking pie and she chocolate cake, and they also brought hot coffee. Annie had worn her best dress and best boots. She kept these items in her wardrobe for only the most important occasions; she was certainly glad she had chosen them tonight. A wonderful day was winding down . . .

Suddenly there was a creak, a groan, and the building was raining plaster, dust, and even bricks. Cal grabbed Annie and pulled her through an exit into the street. All around them people were screaming and running terrified. Annie was horrified herself as she watched buildings crumble and holes begin opening in the street. She remembered thinking: *Is this what hell will be like?* Cal grabbed her hand and pulled her down the street just before a tower came crumbling down. She was in shock! *What is happening? This isn't a hurricane.*

All this was followed by a lull for a few minutes.

"Annie, are you all right?" Cal finally managed to get some words out.

"Yes, but I'm not sure what this is," Annie answered.

But she also often had a nagging, troubling feeling, one of worry about his well-being since she knew his line of work could be risky if he met the wrong people.

"I think it's an earthquake," Cal said, wiping perspiration from his brow. "I've read about these happening. I just never thought I would be in the middle of one." They were walking down the street when they noticed the street lamps had been shattered, that women and children were screaming and sobbing.

Suddenly, there was another shockwave; they felt the ground begin moving. Cal and Annie ran, not even knowing where they were going, just trying to find some sort of safe haven.

"We need to find a safe shelter," Cal said. "Let's go back to our hotel and wait for the dust to settle before we do anything else." Charleston Hotel was only a few blocks down the street, but the walk seemed to take forever. It seemed they could barely see, and they had to be careful where they stepped. There were rocks, dust, and debris everywhere. They made it to the hotel—dusty, dirty, exhausted—and the hotel manager greeted them by name. "Cal, I am glad to see you and Annie made it back," the manager said. "We still have your accommodations, but parts of the hotel have been damaged, so you need to be very careful when leaving your room. Also, we're hearing that many of our citizens here in the city need help. We are forming search and rescue teams to aid those who have been hurt or trapped in the quake."

Cal nodded. "I'm going to escort Annie to our room," he said. Cal took Annie there, and it started to become clear to her what he had in mind. "You're not going back out there, are you?" she asked. He held her close for a minute.

"Annie, I have to go. There are people out there trapped and hurt who may die if someone doesn't help them. I can't just leave those folks out there." She nodded yes, of course; she understood. Cal went on: "You stay here and wait for me. I will return as soon as possible. Don't go out unless you absolutely have to." Again, she nodded. Cal grabbed her hands once more and held them. "I have to go," he said, looking into her eyes.

Annie sat in a chair next to the desk; she would wait for him there. There was no way she could sleep until he returned. She had a few novellas with her, ones she hadn't thought she would have time to read on this trip, so at least this would give her something to do . . .

A bit later, she was tempted to go out and see if there was anything she could do, but she remembered she had promised Cal she would wait.

There were aftershocks several times through the night. She was awakened by one after falling asleep after moving from the desk chair to an easy chair . . .

. . . Someone was tapping at the door. It was well past daylight, and Annie jumped up to find it was Cal. He had brought some sandwiches wrapped in paper. "We helped out many people during the night—some were rescues—and more this morning," he said, looking exhausted and disheveled. "But we are going to have to go out this afternoon and search some more." He paused. "There were some we were too late for. Annie, if you want to help, the hotel kitchen is serving meals for those who've lost their homes." Annie nodded; that would be better than sitting in a room all day by herself, and she truly did want to help.

Cal walked downstairs with her. The kitchen staff was glad for the extra pair of hands. There was no personal or small talk; everything was directed to the damage caused by the earthquake and how people could help. Too many had died (the number wasn't immediately known) or lost their homes; it was a tragic time.

After just a couple of more days, Cal and Annie had to find a buggy, or stage, to take them to a neighboring city from which they could catch their trains, hers to Washington, D.C. and Cal's to head out West. The railroad serving Charleston had been torn apart by the earthquake, and no one knew how long it would take to repair. This had not been the holiday they had planned for; the mayhem and tragedy exhausted them both. It was so hard to say goodbye for both Annie and Cal.

> This had not been the holiday they had planned for; the mayhem and tragedy exhausted them both.

They made plans, but these did not always work out. It seemed like Cal's business— gambling—always came first. They enjoyed their time together before the earthquake, but after the disaster it was a matter of survival and helping others survive. Eventually, it was reported the death toll was between 60 and 100 people. The cost of property damage was unfathomable as almost every building in Charleston was damaged in some way.

Looking back, the worst part for Cal and Annie was when Cal found a badly wounded toddler. He brought the little one to the hotel hoping to find medical help, but the frail child died in his arms.

Annie witnessed this, and it had been too much for her. She could no longer keep her cool façade; she went off to another room to sob uncontrollably. She didn't know if she could survive the news of another death. Seeing this helpless baby—it broke open a deep wound she thought had healed. For his part, Cal also had been almost totally defeated by the event; he placed the baby in the arms of another and went to comfort Annie. Her small body shook; she was sobbing so hard. The whole town smelled of death and destruction—and now a baby. Cal held her in his strong arms and caressed her hair. She had worked so hard to help even though she knew no one in the town; she had given her compassionate and caring best. She was reliving so much pain here in Charleston. Cal was sure this was torture for her.

> Seeing this helpless baby—it broke open a deep wound she thought had healed. For his part, Cal also had been almost totally defeated by the event.

Cal continued to hold her for several quiet moments. Then he spoke softly. "Annie, it's all right. We will be leaving Charleston soon. I'm sorry you had to witness that."

"I'm not crying for myself," Annie said. "I'm crying for the baby and the mother too. These people have suffered so. I have no right to cry when I'm just a bystander." Cal thought to himself that Annie always put on a strong front, never admitting that maybe she needed help as well. He greatly admired that about her.

"Annie, we are not bystanders. This earthquake happened to us both. We were both terrified when it hit, and then when the aftershocks came that was scary too. You have every right to be upset." He stayed with Annie until she calmed down, and then she was ready to return to helping. When Cal questioned Annie, she said, "I have the easy job. You're the one who has been dealing with the danger and the search for survivors or victims." He grabbed her and hugged her tightly before heading back out once more. He was told it was the search party's last sweep, and these had been the most grim chores.

The sun was shining. The dust had finally settled from the quake. Cal and Annie finished packing their bags to head out on a buggy to the nearest town from which they could catch a train. Communications being slow, they weren't sure where they could catch a train, but their driver said he would take them as far as they needed to reach one. He knew all the inns and hotels where they could stay another night if needed, he said.

Cal was determined to make sure Annie arrived in Washington safely. He bought them both a first class ticket, and he would ride the train partway to D.C. before changing trains and heading west. He even made sure to tip the coach-man well so he would continue looking out for Annie on the final leg into D.C.

CHAPTER 13

The Capital: A Brief Season

I'm heading to Washington, D.C., the capital of our country, Annie thought. By the late 1880s, Washington was a fair-sized city with a population of about 132,000. She was on the last leg of her trip on the B&O Railroad; she would be arriving in Washington soon.

The train pulled into a large station on New Jersey Avenue NW, just north of the Capital.[44] Annie's friend in the city had assured her the school would send a buggy, and it was there just as promised. The school board, knowing Annie was there only for a season, had secured a room at a boarding house within walking distance of the school. This was a Young Ladies School and, once again, Annie would be teaching dance.

Annie was excited to be in Washington to help cover for her friend's leave of absence. The appointment worked out perfectly in her schedule and she always wanted to see the nation's capital. Also, the pay was very good, and after the financial catastrophe in Chattanooga, Annie needed to reestablish a stronger savings. She had read that Washington had been in a bad state about ten years ago but had been modernized since.

There were some beautiful buildings in the city: the National Museum, the Agriculture Department, and the Sumner and Franklin schools. And, of course, the Capitol building and White House. (Many of these buildings had been designed by a German immigrant, Adolf Cluss.[45]) She couldn't wait to see the Washington Monument, a tribute to George Washington and the world's tallest stone structure, which had been completed just a couple of years before. In fact, the first thing Annie did after settling in the boarding house was take a long walk to see the Monument before the weather turned bad. It did not disappoint; it was one of the most amazing manmade objects she had seen.[46]

It was a mild winter, and her time here went by fast. Annie's short walk in the morning from the boarding house to the school was just enough to help her catch her first wind. The pay was good, but she was lonely here. The people weren't as friendly as they were in Asheville. By the time her winter/spring appointment was done, Annie was ready to go.

> The pay was good, but she was lonely here. The people weren't as friendly as they were in Asheville.

Her best friend from childhood, Emily Brown, who she had not seen in several years, had invited her to Auburn, New York for the summer and fall, although she told Annie she was welcome to stay as long as she liked. For now, Annie looked forward to seeing Emily, spending quiet evenings by the fire, visiting with her, and reminiscing about times when life was easier and so much simpler.

She so badly wanted to tell Emily about her adventures, the sights she had seen, and most of all, about Cal.

CHAPTER 14

Almost Like Home

Emily Brown, Annie's best friend from childhood, was a schoolteacher like Annie had been. But unlike Annie, she led a quiet, staid life. Emily lived in a small cottage past the edge of town, located on a couple of acres, next to the woods. She had some chickens for fresh eggs and a nice garden that provided vegetables all summer that she canned in the fall.

Annie needed this time, and her best friend. Emily was one of the few links she had to her once carefree childhood and her late parents. It was restful up here in Auburn. People knew Annie as a schoolteacher, as they did Emily. There were no questions, they were just accepted as two old maid schoolteachers (even though Annie was a widow; Emily had never married). Annie did not wish to talk about her circumstances with strangers or even most of her family or friends.

Annie and Emily would enjoy a simple but nice dinner by the fireside every evening, clean up the dishes, and then converse or read for a bit. She enjoyed the tiny guest bedroom; it was private, nice. Emily had put a vase of fresh-cut lilacs in her room on the side of her dressing table. The room smelled so nice with freshly washed linens on her bed and the lilacs, and she also had a colorful handmade quilt to keep her warm. Emily had been able to keep the beautiful, hand-embroidered pillow covers her mother had made. She placed one of the pillow covers on Annie's pillow, which meant so much to Annie; she also placed one of her mother's hand-embroidered dresser scarves on the small dresser in Annie's room. There was a nice rag rug next to Annie's bed so that when she got out of bed her feet wouldn't get cold on the wooden floor. And next to her bed was a nice bedstand with a kerosene lamp. The hand-embroidered linen curtains on her window also had been freshly washed, and, again, these were some that Emily's mother had embroidered.

Annie knew Emily had gone to a lot of trouble. For instance, these linens were generally kept in a chest where the sunlight couldn't fade them or a spill could not ruin them. When Annie had been sent to boarding school all those years ago, she was only given a handkerchief of her mother's and a piece of her jewelry. Sadly, both were lost in the Chattanooga housefire. And Annie greatly enjoyed only having to share a bathroom with one person and not having to worry about peeping toms.

At night Annie would open her window, let the cool breezes in, and enjoy the gentle rays of moonlight through the window. In the summer, when Emily wasn't working, they enjoyed walking in the woods, looking for berries, and identifying various kinds of trees and flowers as they did when they were children. Annie enjoyed helping her friend can the vegetables she had grown in her garden and the berries they had found. She enjoyed the smell of the fresh vegetables as they cut them up and put them in the jars, and the rattle of the jars boiling on the stove. She especially loved the smell of the black raspberries as they cooked down for jam. The jam itself, on homemade biscuits, was absolutely heavenly. All these tasks made Annie feel productive and gave her the knowledge that, in a small way, she had helped her best friend out after all Emily did for her that summer.

Her heart still ached for them; tears would run down her cheeks looking at their lonely graves.

Summer flew by quickly, and when Emily went back to teaching school in the fall, Annie continued her walks in the woods and enjoyed the quiet. She also visited with family while in Auburn and—among her most precious times—visited her dear husband's and son's graves. Her heart still ached for them; tears would run down her cheeks looking at their lonely graves.

One evening after dinner, Emily finally asked the personal question Annie had wondered for many weeks might be coming. "Annie, do you have anyone, a beau, in your life?" That opened up the conversation Annie had been wanting to have with her best friend.

"Yes, yes, I do. His name is Calvin. Everyone calls him Cal. And he is so handsome." Annie proceeded to tell Emily all about Calvin. She was so happy to get it all out. But then, in a moment of recognition, she looked at her best friend's face. Annie read that Emily had someone too. "Do you have a beau?"

"Yes I do," Emily said. "He's a quiet man. He's away on a job this summer but will be coming back this fall. We take long walks and talk. He is so kind and such a good companion, and he is pretty protective of me." Annie felt a sense of relief after Emily told her this news. Annie liked the idea of her friend having someone to watch out for her, of her not being all alone. "Hopefully you will still be here when he returns," Emily said. "I would love for you to meet him." Annie smiled at that thought.

The two friends went to bed that night with a sense of relief and a feeling of closeness they had not felt before. Both had needed to talk of these things with the other.

Even though Annie loved it at her best friend's place, she was relieved and excited when she received a letter from a Young Ladies School in Lafayette, Indiana to which she had sent an application for a teaching position in dance. Emily had been hoping Annie could find a position closer to her, and she was disappointed for herself but happy for Annie when Annie told her the news. She knew Annie couldn't stay forever, but she had cherished the brief time they had together. She had been, like Annie, lonely and enjoyed Annie's company over the summer. "Annie, I will miss you when you leave," Emily sighed with sadness.

"I will miss you too," Annie replied. "If the world was a simpler, easier place to live in . . . " Annie let the words trail off, their meaning clear. "But I have my calling and you have yours." *Why does life have to be so complicated?*, Annie thought. Why couldn't things remain black and white like she was led to believe when she was little? Annie sometimes felt like she was

Annie sometimes felt like she was lost in the grays of life, in its shadows and clouds. It felt as if the sun had stopped shining for her a long time ago.

lost in the grays of life, in its shadows and clouds. It felt as if the sun had stopped shining for her a long time ago.

Annie's stay in the small Indiana town teaching dance was uneventful. She kept in regular touch with Emily and Cal—and with her older sister and younger brothers she did have a relationship with, to a lesser extent—through letters. She spent the following summer, an uneventful one, in Sault Ste. Marie, Michigan, teaching a system of piano music.[47] She liked Sault Ste. Marie. It was a little river town, although a very important one. Full of hustle and bustle, the St. Mary's River served as the only connection between Lake Superior and the other Great Lakes. Having somewhat of a scientific mind, she found the Weitzel Lock and how it worked fascinating. That these great ships could be moved through the river and back out to Lake Superior by a series of locks that filled and emptied through the chamber floors was utterly amazing to her.

When she returned to Indiana that fall, the fall of 1888, she received a letter from Cal asking that she travel with him to San Antonio and then on to Mexico City for the month of December. They could celebrate Christmas together, Cal wrote, and then head back to San Antonio.

This time she would be able to take a train to San Antonio to meet Cal, and from there they would ride together on a train to Mexico City. Altogether the trip would take about three months. Annie once again grew greatly excited; she and Cal hadn't spent any time together since Charleston and that horrible earthquake. She gave notice for her position at the Lafayette dance school; she knew they wouldn't give her extended vacation in the middle of the school year. She did not want to have to explain where she was going and why.

CHAPTER 15

Poinsettias in Mexico

It was late 1888. Annie was excited and hoping at last for a proposal of marriage. She packed her nicest clothes—what she had, anyway. She would be traveling by rail to San Antonio. It would be a scenic trip as she would be able to view the countryside from Indiana down to Texas, but it would also be a very long and tiring trip, one taking about a week and a half with many stops in small towns.[49] Annie would be traveling on the Galveston, Harrisburg, and San Antonio railways. San Antonio was one of the fastest growing cities in the U.S. and suddenly one of its most modern. Annie was excited to see how much San Antonio had grown since she had last been here.[50] While there she and Cal would be staying at the Menger Hotel, known as one of the nicest hotels not only in San Antonio but in the entire Southwest; it was located adjacent to the famous Alamo. The Menger was praised for its cuisine "offered in the Colonial Dining Room, which included such specialties as wild game, mango ice cream, and snapper soup."[51] When Annie lived in San Antonio years ago she heard a great deal about the Menger and its famous clientele. (Annie thought about visiting the Kingsbury sisters while in San Antonio, but she had failed to keep in touch with them through the years. She felt asking for a visit, years later, might be awkward.)

She and Cal would later travel by rail to Mexico City. There was now a completed railway system in Mexico, the Mexican National and the Mexican Central railroads. This would make that trip so much easier.[52]

Annie knew they would be staying in the best of hotels in Mexico City and eating at the finest restaurants. Cal also took pride in taking her shopping and buying Annie fine clothes for the trip. Sometimes Annie felt guilty about what he spent on her knowing he had won the money in a game of faro or monte from some poor soul not as gifted as himself. She soothed her conscience, though, by telling herself that that person had made the decision to willingly gamble. Cal was the only one she loved, Annie knew, and she was the only one he loved.

Annie had been terribly lonely in Indiana; she didn't know many people. The mothers of her students all considered themselves of a higher-class status than she, so social invitations were few and far between. The other teachers at the

> The mothers of her students all considered themselves of a higher-class status than she, so social invitations were few and far between. She was the outcast, the outsider, as she had been so many times before.

school had known each other for a long time, so they had friendships she was not invited into. She was the outcast, the outsider, as she had been so many times before. It was without regret that Annie submitted her resignation to the head of the school. The head school marm was upset; she had no idea if she would be able to replace Annie on such short notice, especially in the middle of the holidays (Thanksgiving was coming soon), or even by the second semester. But a twinge of guilt reminded the headmistress that they had not been kind to Annie at all and had not planned on being so. Annie was regarded as an old maid schoolteacher; no one had sincerely inquired into her past, her personal life. The head marm was a little mystified, though; she had never seen Annie so happy in the entire time she taught there. She inquired in a hinting sort of way as to what Annie's plans were, but Annie was close-mouthed and just said, "personal business."

The rail trip to San Antonio was, for the most part, tiring. Traveling through Indiana and Kansas was monotonous, but Annie did love the expanse, the desolation of the western prairie, and the tall prairie grass of western Kansas. Although Missouri was scenic (there were more hills and valleys), Oklahoma was all farms and ranches. Then down through Northern Texas, through hill country to San Antonio. Annie had loved San Antonio when she was there before, but since the railroad had come through, it had grown quite a bit. Things had changed a great deal since then.

Arriving at the San Antonio station, she frantically looked for Cal. Finally she spotted him, leaning against a door, vigilantly watching for her. A big smile broke across Cal's face as soon as he saw her. He ran up and gave her a huge hug;

Annie was laughing and smiling. She instantly knew she had not laughed or even smiled like that in a very long time.

"How's my precious Annie?" Cal asked. She just smiled and hugged him back. "I'm fine now that I'm with you. But how are you doing?" As always, Cal answered with confidence. "Very well, thank you. I have a coach waiting for us outside to take us to our hotel next to the Alamo." Calvin knew Annie would love staying there as she enjoyed historic, glamorous places. She nodded. "I'm ready."

On the way to the hotel Annie chattered the whole time about her trip into Texas. Cal was a good listener, and he later chatted some about his journey from Denver. Their buggy went slowly past the Alamo as the driver pointed out the historic structure. After Cal checked in at the Menger Hotel, he told Annie she had the room to herself for the afternoon since he had a scheduled a game of faro. He would meet her, he said, for dinner in the Colonial Dining Room at 7 p.m.[53] However, the game of faro was really a cover. Calvin had set up an appointment to finalize his buying a small ranch outside of San Antonio; this was one of two surprises he had for Annie. For her part, Annie found herself relieved to be able to clean up after such an arduous trip. She laid out her Sunday best and her most up-to-date boots.

Their stay in San Antonio pretty much went that way for the next week. Cal was in high-stakes poker, monte, or faro games, Annie resting, reading, and waiting for their dinner and evenings together. For the most part, Cal fared well in his gambling that week.

Soon it was time for their journey to Mexico City. It too would be by rail, which was much better than traveling by stagecoach. The weather, fortunately, was fair, so Annie enjoyed the scenery on the way down. She did, however, miss traveling by ship as she enjoyed walking the deck and looking out at the Gulf of Mexico during the trip from Cuba to Galveston. To her great happiness, though, Cal had no games set up on the train; they were able to eat nice meals in the dining car and enjoy the journey together. The trip went smoothly and without problems.

Once they crossed into Mexico they were served a different cuisine, and Annie and Cal both enjoyed the Mexican food. It was well worth the long trip, and they arrived in mid-November; the weather was perfect, mid-70s every day. The Americans who were vacationing or there for business weren't into gambling much. The Mexicans? They were more into betting on cockfights than card gambling.

To Annie's delight, her and Cal's time was usually filled with sightseeing and shopping. They were able to enjoy leisurely breakfasts and morning and evening walks. Annie spent much more time with Cal in Mexico than she had been able to in Texas. All the food was excellent, but at dinner the meals were especially delightful, a good deal of fresh fish and seafood served with Sangria, and every night the mariachi bands sang and played their music on the string guitars and trombones. It was so romantic. Sometimes they would try another restaurant besides their hotel restaurant, but the service and food were best there.

Best of all, there was no one poking their nose in their business. It was just locals or employees wishing them a pleasant stay. Every day after the maid straightened their room there were flower petals sprinkled on the bed and a towel left in the shape of a bird or goose. When needed, the flower vase by the window would sport freshly cut flowers that filled the room with wonderful scents. Annie loved Cal so much, and this was the first time in a long time they had really been together, relaxed and laughing, enjoying their days together. The stress was melting away, and Annie felt better than she had in a very long time.

In the late 1880s General Porfirio Diaz[54] was the president of Mexico. Although he ruled with an iron fist, he had brought some positive changes. Diaz established order and a workable government. Civil wars ceased and banditry disappeared from the countryside. Foreign investment rushed in to take advantage of the new political and economic climates. This revived mining and created major oil fields. Exports and national income increased, and new industries dotted the countryside. Something Cal very much wanted to share with Annie was the Christmas Celebration in Mexico City. Mexicans typically celebrate Christmas from early December through January 6.[55]

> There were elaborate nativity scenes in many locations, some covered with Spanish moss, and some featuring churches, musicians, dancers, playing children, and vendors.

When Cal and Annie awoke in Mexico City one morning in early December, overnight the city had been transformed with beautiful poinsettias and lit candles decorating every home. The Zocalo (town square) was bright with red poinsettias. The streets were bustling with stalls selling decorations, several types of gifts, and, of course, poinsettias, which were often called Noche Buena (from the Spanish phrase "good night," referring to Christmas Eve). The streets were filled with Mexican Christmas music such as "Los

Pastores a Belen" and "Riu, Riu, Chiu: El Lobo Rabioso." They were sung by groups of adults and children. There were elaborate nativity scenes in many locations, some covered with Spanish moss, and some featuring churches, musicians, dancers, playing children, and vendors with carts of fruit and vegetables. All this activity surrounded, of course, the central feature, the Holy Family. The only thing missing was the Christ child, and he was placed in the nativity scenes on Christmas Eve.[56]

Annie had never witnessed such a totally festive atmosphere as Mexico City that Christmas season. Her family had always celebrated Christmas, but her Christmases at the boarding school and the Albany State School for Teachers had been very low-key, even staid affairs. The best Christmases she could remember were with Samuel during their short marriage; though not elaborate, the small gifts they gave each other meant so much. But in Mexico, Annie had never seen anything like this, and she was utterly amazed. Cal chuckled knowing that the celebrations would go on through January 6, and the Christmas Eve revelry, he knew, was the most festive and joyous of all.

Cal had hoped to add joy to Annie's life; she worked so hard and had waited so patiently for him. Life had been, too often, harsh for Annie. It hurt Cal to see her suddenly hit with grief over the loss of her parents, husband, and son; she deserved to dance and sing, he told himself.

What a fine place and time to be alive, each there with the other, in Mexico City in December 1888.

They had been settled into their hotel for a few weeks and had gotten used to the city when Cal asked Annie if she would be interested in an excursion outside of Mexico City. When he explained that they would be traveling to see ancient pyramids Annie was immediately fascinated. Cal laughed seeing the delight in her eyes. "You're like a young child going to her first circus," he told her. He hugged her and told her how special she was. He knew how lucky he was to find her. And Annie? She was just in awe of him.

CHAPTER 16

A Special Christmas

A few days later they took a stagecoach to the mysterious Teotihuacan Pyramids.[57] The trip had been arranged by a government official who was a good friend of some of the businessmen and gamblers Cal knew. There were four stagecoaches: three for the tourist party and the fourth for supplies for their picnic at the site and the people who would be preparing and serving the food. They would spend one night there overnight. They were also accompanied by four fully armed guards on horseback. The whole trip, Annie realized, was quite a big deal.

Once there, Annie was totally fascinated with the pyramids and their mysterious history. These pyramids were, according to various sources, "inexplicably abandoned centuries before the arrival of the Aztecs, who called the ancient architectural marvel the 'Birthplace of the Gods.' . . . These massive ruins are presided over by the third-largest pyramid in the world, which was constructed according to precise astronomical measurements and filled with the bodies of sacrificial victims.

. . . Some of the temples were still covered with rich and detailed stone statues, even faded paintings." Annie felt like a girl again; these pyramids greatly piqued her curiosity. This had to be one of the most fascinating sights she had ever seen. Cal was just as excited as Annie if not more. He too found the mystery of the pyramids fascinating.

With all the walking the trek involved, Cal and Annie were both well ahead of everyone (other than the guide) as both were in excellent physical shape. (This athleticism was, perhaps, a precursor, an early sign, of the agility she would need for her famous Falls stunt—still nearly thirteen years in her future.) Even though they were doing so well with the hike, Annie was glad when they sat down for their lunch. Huge pitchers of lime-aid and Sangria were served, and both she and Cal were quite thirsty. The men were offered little pitchers of tequila as well, though Cal quietly let his sit.

Both were exhausted from a physical day when they reached their hotel that evening, and they agreed they would just have the hotel bring up a light snack. Neither was up to dressing well and heading down to dinner.

After returning to Mexico City, it was nearly Christmas Eve. This one day is a special time in Mexico.[58] According to sources, "The last posada [festive gathering] is early Christmas Eve. What follows is a late night mass called the Mass of the Rooster. The name comes from the tradition that the birth of Christ was announced by the crowing of a rooster. . . . The celebration became popular among the newly converted indigenous [peoples] as it included elements from the old celebrations for the god Huitzilopochtli such as fireworks, torches, sparklers, plays, food, and dancing. . . . Following the mass, there is a traditional midnight feast. Traditional dishes include bacalao [a type of cod], reconstituted dried cod cooked with onions, tomato sauce, olives, and more. Another is *revoltijo deromerita*, which is green chilies in a mole of pepita sauce, with potatoes and often dried shrimp. The most luxurious item on the menu [is] suckling pig. After dinner adults drink ponche or cider and children play with sparklers, called Luces de Belen [Bethlehem Nights]. . . . Christmas presents are usually opened at the stroke of midnight."

And then, traditionally, the rest of Christmas Day is quiet in Mexico as families recuperate from the festivities the night before.

For Cal, this night had another meaning. This was the night he was going to propose to Annie and present her with the deed to a ranch outside San Antonio. He was going to give her a beautiful diamond engagement ring. This was sure to be a Christmas Eve neither would forget.

First, they attended mass at a nearby church. The hotel where they were staying was having a wonderful feast afterward; the main course was, once again, suckling pig. After the feast there was dancing, singing, and much celebrating.

> Although they had been unofficially engaged for a long time, Cal had never made things official. Now, finally, was the time to take that step.

As a Christmas gift, while they were still in San Antonio, Cal had bought Annie the piece of land he had been eyeing for some time. He intended that, once they had enough savings, they would get married, settle down, and hopefully raise a family on this ranch. Although they had been unofficially engaged for a long time, Cal had never made things official. Now, finally, was the time to take that step.

After the feast Cal and Annie headed to the hotel ballroom; it was festively decorated. Annie looked beautiful in a blue satin dress and black leather ankle boots; her thick brown hair was swept into an updo. Cal asked her to dance even though they did not know all the words to the songs. They joined the floor and danced lightheartedly, sharing the delight of being together. Finally, they were both out of breath and laughing. Cal looked at Annie and said, "Let's step outside for some fresh air. I really need to cool off." Annie nodded yes, that she was out of breath too, and they went out to the courtyard under a beautiful shining moon.

Annie looked at Cal admiringly and said, "What a beautiful evening. This is such a wonderful Christmas Eve celebration." And then . . . Calvin did it. He knelt before Annie and took her hand. "Annie, you are the love of my life and the most patient woman I have ever met. Will you marry me?" Annie was breathless as she nodded yes, her face shining with happiness and joy. Cal pulled out a beautiful gold ring with a dazzling one-karat diamond. Annie had never seen a ring so beautiful. He slipped the ring on her finger, grabbed her, and kissed her passionately.

Cal stepped back and took a breath. "One more surprise," he said. Annie just blushed while saying, "I don't know if I can handle another surprise. You just gave me the most wonderful Christmas gift ever." Cal slowly pulled out a piece of paper rolled up and tied with a red ribbon. He told Annie to open it, and when she did, and quickly read its contents, she let out a whoop, hugged him, and kissed him. "I'm so sorry. That was so unladylike," she said, laughing. "I was so surprised. This is wonderful. Is this deed for the land for our ranch we talked about?" Cal said that indeed it was, that when they were married the two of them could build a home and start a ranch on this land.

Annie had to stop for a moment to think. "What will we do with the land in the meantime?" she asked.

"The rancher that sold me the land will use it to graze his cattle, and watch over it, until we can set up a ranch," Cal said. "He is a good man and is good on his word. No need to worry."

Annie looked up at the moonlight. Everything seemed too good to be true. "Thank you. Does this mean that we really have a future together?" she whispered.

Cal nodded. "Someday." He took her in his arms and gave her a long kiss and then just held her. "You have been so faithful to me for so long, when I have given you nothing, not even promises," he said. "I felt you deserved this." Deep inside, Cal was thinking he should have made Annie his wife a long time ago. But he also knew that he really didn't have the money, and being a professional gambler was a very risky way of life.

Some of the places Cal went to earn a living were nothing more than mudholes with a shack or two stuck up around them, and there was little to no law out West. He didn't want to expose Annie to the saloons and brothels he frequented. These were not places for an educated lady and especially not for a beautiful woman he hoped to make his wife someday.

Cal took another breath while gazing up at the moonlight. "May I dance with my fiancée one more time before we retire?" Cal whisked her off to the dance floor.

All in all, it was one of the most wonderful Christmases Annie ever had.

CHAPTER 17

Au Revoir for Now

Cal and Annie boarded the Texas-Mexican Railway on January 2, 1889, and headed back to El Paso on the other side of the U.S. border, where they would change to the Santa Fe Railroad. The trip was 737 miles from Mexico City to Nuevo Laredo and then, across the border, lay the Laredo Port of Entry in Webb County, Texas.[59] Then it was on to San Antonio and home from there.

The trip went too fast for Annie, but by the end, Cal was anxious to get back. He had some high dollar games he had previously set up, and he found himself eager to get back to his business. He and Annie had a wonderful, relaxing holiday together, the best he had had in a very long time. He felt rested and renewed, and Annie glowed like a young woman of about 20 who was in love for the first time. Cal loved seeing his Annie like this knowing the ugly burdens life had placed on her at such a youthful age. But he also felt a twinge of guilt because he knew she had another period of waiting before they could marry. Still, Cal felt much better knowing Annie had the deed to the ranch, and knowing they had a plan.

It was a peaceful trip back to Texas, the January skies as clear as they had seen, the stars bright, the landscape peaceful. Annie and Cal both felt as if they were in a dream. The hustle and bustle at the Port of Entry in Laredo took both their minds off the inevitable separation that was coming. Next it was on to San Antonio by train and, from there, a goodbye neither of them was looking forward to.

Despite all this, Annie maintained a secret worry about Cal. He seemed to push too hard at his craft, traveling to dangerous places and associating with dangerous people.

Before those goodbyes, Annie and Cal spent a final day together and took a stagecoach to the ranch land he had bought her. The land was still wild and untamed. The only way she could ever settle there was if Cal was with her. As Annie surveyed the lush but forbidding countryside, she hoped the ranch would be a reality someday and not just a dream for an empty parcel of land.

She cried when they finally said goodbye. She was certain they had grown closer than they ever had been.

Despite all this, Annie maintained a secret worry about Cal. He seemed to push too hard at his craft, traveling to dangerous places and associating with dangerous people. Men who would shoot another at the drop of a hat—and, too often, no law around to protect the innocent.

CHAPTER 18

Back to Michigan . . .
and Stunning News

Annie had decided this was her time to return to Michigan. The train trip north was most dreary, and she dreaded going back there, but she really had nowhere else to go. She had made arrangements to once again occupy the little house in Bay City she had inherited through Samuel's estate. She had contacted a local minister there[60] to help smooth her way back into Bay City society. She was hoping her stay would be short, that she would be back in Texas with Cal soon.

Annie still had a few friends left in Bay City who, despite the gossip about her many travels, supported her in her endeavors. These friends had been close to her and Samuel and realized how much Annie loved and cared for him and their son, and the depth of her grief, what she went through when she lost her family at such an early age. She still would cry when she thought about Samuel and her son; it was as if her heart was being ripped out all over again. She knew she would never stop grieving for them.

Annie had finally cleaned enough to put her little house in order. It was a pleasant little cottage, not big but comfortable for her. She did have enough room to install indoor plumbing, and this was such a comfort. The house had a nice porch to sit on and a small but well-kept yard. She started the process of setting up classes in physical culture for young ladies at the high school. She had been very busy and yet content with how much she accomplished in such a brief time.

Still, her life with Cal awaited her, and she was hoping she would hear from him soon. When she did, at the right time, she could sell this house to help finance building their new home on their ranch.

Not long into her stay in Bay City, there was a knock at her door one afternoon; this was unusual for the time of day. Annie peeked out the window, but all she could see was a nice carriage; she didn't know who this was. She answered the door and instantly recognized a friend of Calvin's; his name was Ezekiel Good. Annie had met Ezekiel a couple of times in San Antonio. He had a sad, tired look on his face and took his hat off as soon as Annie answered the door. "Annie, may I come in for a moment?" Ezekiel asked.

Annie welcomed him in, of course, but suddenly she had a very bad feeling; this was not normal. She motioned for Ezekiel to sit down, and then she took a seat. He swallowed. "Annie, I don't know how to say this, but Cal is gone." He looked down, paused. "He was shot in the heart—over a game of monte. He had won a very large amount of money and was getting ready to leave when the other man drew his gun and shot him." He paused again. "He had no warning, no chance to defend himself."

Annie clasped her hand over her mouth. She felt like she was going to throw up; she ran into the kitchen and started heaving in the wastebasket. After a few minutes, she wiped her face with a cloth and went back in her sitting room, but she couldn't say a word. She just started sobbing.

"I'm so, so sorry," Ezekiel said. "I know you and Cal were engaged to be married, and all he talked about was winning a nice nest egg so you two could get married and set up your ranch." Annie nodded, but she couldn't look at the man. Her head hurt. *How could this happen?* Just when she thought they might have a future together. Finally, she composed herself and asked Ezekiel, her voice in a whisper, "What was done with his body?"

Ezekiel swallowed hard once more. "He was buried in an unmarked grave. I was not there to claim the body. After he was declared dead, they placed him in a wooden coffin, had a short service, and buried him."

Annie was numb. "Thank you for coming and relaying the news," she said. "I can't chat with you right now. I have a terrible headache."

He nodded. "I must go anyway. I'm leaving you my card. I will be in town a few days at this hotel. If you need anything, please let me know." He hesitated, then added, "I beg your pardon. I know this is quite a shock, but there is one other matter I must take care of while I'm here." He pulled a large roll of money from his pocket. "This money was meant for you, Annie. If you are frugal, it should last you a while." Annie simply whispered, "Thank you."

Ezekiel left quietly, and Annie locked the door behind him. She was numb; there was nothing left inside her. She went to bed and didn't get up for five days except for brief periods of getting something small to eat. No one came by, no one knew. She hoped if anyone stopped they would simply think she wasn't home. Annie had no desire to talk to anyone. She just slept and cried. She took medicine for her headache, but it didn't seem to help.

Finally, on the sixth day, she got out of bed. "There is no feeling sorry for yourself," she said numbly to herself. And she swore to herself that she would never fall in love again. Two men were more than enough for her lifetime, she was sure. First her beloved Samuel, whom she lost so suddenly, and also her dear son; she would never stop mourning either of them. And now . . . Cal. She felt so blessed when he had proposed marriage to her and gave her the deed to the ranch. She had been daydreaming of their new home, of returning to Texas permanently. She loved it there, and now that dream was gone as well. Now she was left with nothing, just her little house here in Bay City. Her life felt like grains of sand that had run through her fingers—nothing was left but a few pebbles of memories.

That morning was a Sunday, and Annie got dressed for church. It was also this morning that she made up her mind not to fall in love again, to dedicate herself to the church, to helping others as much as she could, and to teaching physical culture and dance at the local school. She would live thriftily;

no more travel. Any extra money she had, she decided, would go to charity.

Also, she made up her mind to attend church every Sunday. She wanted to get right with God.

Her Falls attempt was still a dozen years away.

Annie lived like this for many years: pinching pennies, wearing her clothes and shoes until they were worn out, working at the school, helping at church. Most of her social life was through the church or school; otherwise, she had very little of it. Mostly, she kept to herself. Her entertainment at home was reading. She had always been an avid reader, enjoying books and the newspaper. She afforded herself the luxury of a good ladies' cigar now and again—that was her only vice. The smoking brought back memories of her time in Asheville and the Swannanoa Hotel, the bright summer days teaching hotel residents to dance, the evenings spent with friends who, like her, had gone through a rough time and were just happy to be working in such a lovely place. In short, talking, laughing, and sharing a smoke between teaching this one and that one to dance. It had been such a congenial atmosphere, so light-hearted and fun.

Then came her time with Cal. He thought it was sophisticated, Annie smoking her little cigars. Sometimes when he would return from his travels he would bring her a box of an exclusive brand that came from Cuba. He would smile and give her a big wink when she lit up.

Annie would end her days by quietly getting ready for bed. There was no sense worrying over what might have been, she told herself. Other times, with tears, she would remember her beloved Samuel and their son. These were the tough nights when she would pour herself a small glass of wine for comfort and sleep. She tried not to think about Calvin, but her love for him, and his love for her, had been very real too. What was meant to be would be, and she left it there.

The years seemed to go by quickly. Annie had gotten herself in debt. Two good friends of hers—one widowed with small children, the other friend ill—both needed financial help.

It was at this point that Annie had an epiphany about the Falls.[61]

* * * * *

> The years seemed to go by quickly. Annie had gotten herself in debt.

Again, a knock at her door.

"Annie, it's time. Time for you to do this, if you are ready." Frank Russell was at her door, knocking impatiently. He was ready for this act to be performed; they had already gone past the time set for the stunt.[62] The men with the boat were ready. Better to do it now before someone loses their nerve and everything falls apart, Russell knew. He had done a lot of work on this, drumming up publicity, getting the boat set up with two rivermen who knew the dangerous waters, who weren't afraid of the law, and who had the nerve to be part of this effort.

In one very real sense, Annie was excited. But she felt a bit numb, too, as she thought back over her life. She had made a lot of mistakes—but she also knew *God* had made a difference in her life, had carried her through the roughest patches.

Annie said a quick prayer: she asked for His grace, mercy, and safety.

She felt better now. She was ready to go, to show the world what little Annie, the daredevil, was really made of.

CHAPTER 19

The Falls

Annie ended this reminiscing about her life. It was as if she had needed to review her entire life before she went forward with this next step.

Hopefully, if she was successful in her attempt, she would become rich and famous. If not, she knew full well, she could be killed or crippled for life. The latter bothered her more than the former; in dying, she believed, she would be with her dear Samuel and their sweet son again. Crippled, she would be dependent on the kindness and charity of others, and she dreaded that thought since people hadn't always been so kind or charitable to her.

Annie said one final prayer. Then she stepped out of her quarters on First Street in Niagara Falls, New York. She quickly entered the closed carriage with her manager already aboard, and it didn't take long to transport her to the shore of the upper Niagara. Already, she knew, she was running late. When she arrived where the rowboat was docked, there was a gathering of well-wishers and reporters. Russell, her manager, began shaking hands and talking with everyone, but many were there simply to wave goodbye to Annie and wish her the best of luck.

Annie gave the briefest of speeches. "No, I will not say goodbye, but au revoir. I will see you in fifty minutes, below the cataract."[63] Russell did not look concerned; he just smiled and waved. Still, both were well aware they were twenty-five minutes behind the publicly announced schedule, so there was pressure to get going, and this to perform an incredibly dangerous stunt.

Annie quickly boarded the rowboat. The rivermen rowed her out to Grass Island, which lies about one and one-half miles above Horseshoe Falls. Annie sent the men away for a few moments so she could take off her heavy outer clothes and fit comfortably into the barrel, which she had built back in Michigan for the attempt. The men tightly sealed the barrel, then lowered it in the water. They took one last step, pumping the barrel full of air so she wouldn't suffocate from lack of oxygen while inside.

The time was upon her, and Annie felt her throat tightening. She had to catch her breath and force herself to remain calm. She could no longer hear people on the shore. Now there was only darkness and the sound of her heart beating. Annie realized this barrel could, within minutes, be the coffin she would find herself buried in at the bottom of the Falls.

The time had come. When the rivermen saw the barrel start floating, they cut the rope attached to it and at the same time rapped loudly on the barrel to let Annie know she was now on her own.

There was no denying to herself that Annie was now frightened after she was closed in the barrel and realized it had been cut loose. She calmed herself by saying still another prayer and asking God to do one of two things: let her survive without serious injury or let her die an instant death.

But then, within moments, she felt surprise at her next sensation: she felt a peace, an actual *enjoyment*, going down the river. It actually stirred in her a calming sensation. She let the rolling of the barrel and sound of the river lull her into a serene state of mind . . .

The time had come. When the rivermen saw the barrel start floating, they cut the rope attached to it and at the same time rapped loudly on the barrel.

Then, without warning, the barrel swerved, nearly causing a state of panic as she thought she would be going down the Falls headfirst into the rocks below; this would surely kill her. But as if guided by the hand of Providence, the barrel swerved again, just in time to head over the Falls—feet first. From her inside perch, she could feel the barrel rise to the surface as it headed toward the edge of the Falls; she knew this put her in the position of going over feet first.

Quickly, Annie made a decision: she tore the cushion away that was protecting her head and placed it under her knees. The barrel slowed for a few brief moments before reaching the edge of Horseshoe Falls. Then Annie's throat tightened; she knew the real test was coming within seconds. This plunge could mean her last breath, her final thoughts as a mortal on this earth . . .

This could be her final goodbye—although everyone she truly loved had gone before her. Maybe now she would join them. She would leave that to God. . . .

As the barrel dropped over the edge, Annie was surrounded by deafening sound, the roar of the magnificent Falls she was hoping to conquer. She was enveloped in that sound as if held captive by it. The roar going over the Falls was so loud and intense; she could think of nothing else, just being in that moment. . . .

And then she felt a return to her senses when the barrel hit the lower river. The silence now was haunting after the deafening roar of the Falls.

> As the barrel dropped over the edge, Annie was surrounded by deafening sound, the roar of the magnificent Falls she was hoping to conquer.

She instinctively knew she was below the water and had survived the plunge. But when would the barrel resurface?

Then, to her terror, the momentum of the water from the Falls threw her barrel *behind* the great cascade of water. The force of the water tossed the barrel about violently and recklessly as if it was angry at her presence, that she dare challenge this mighty force of nature. The barrel was caught in the tumultuous waters behind the Falls, twirling her small vessel about as if it was a toy. Annie found herself getting nauseous and dizzy from the twirling motion. It was as if she was on a runaway carnival ride—only one much faster and incredibly dangerous. Suddenly, the turbulent waves were actually lifting the barrel four or five feet in the air.

Knowing she was behind the Falls, Annie was fully aware that no one could help her. And then, in a moment, as in the snap of a finger, the Falls shot the barrel out into the river, as if it had been fired from a cannon. It caused her to reel from the impact when the barrel hit the water. In what seemed like a lifetime the barrel floated farther down the river, but in actuality this last trip lasted only a few minutes. Miraculously, Annie felt the barrel resting on a rock. She breathed a sigh of relief. The journey was over. She was safe!

After the stress of going over the Falls and realizing she would soon be rescued, Annie felt her consciousness slip away. When her rescuers opened the barrel the shock of the cool, fresh air brought her back to her senses. What a sweet moment. It was over. She had survived!

Watching the barrel take its plunge must have been both intriguing and terrifying to its audience, which had no idea what the forces of nature had in store for Annie and her vessel. Nature can be kind, but also extremely cruel, and the power of Horseshoe Falls was nothing to be toyed with. From their perspective, they had watched the barrel drop over[64] the Falls and then sink below the water but just as quickly be shot back into the air, only to then be swept behind the Falls. Then, stunned, they saw that, miraculously, the barrel had been thrown out by some rocks and floated to safety before finally getting hung up on downriver rocks.

The workmen quickly grabbed the barrel, opened it, and peered inside. To their great relief Annie was alive and gasping for air. Someone exclaimed, "The woman is alive!" Annie delivered a short response: "Yes, she is."

To everyone's astonishment Annie walked to the shore on her own power, though she did accept the aid of being helped across a few rocks. Everyone was celebrating. Annie was placed in a carriage and taken back to the boarding house where she had been staying.

She didn't remember a great deal after that, though she did remember a doctor checking on her a few days later. But she did recall this: the sounds of whistles blowing, bells ringing, and people cheering.

She was seen as a hero. Annie Taylor had conquered the Falls!

CHAPTER 20

High Hopes Dashed

After her ride over Horseshoe Falls, for a brief period Annie was a much sought-after speaker. There was a public reception for her on Farewell Day at the Pan-American Exposition. She didn't speak that day but accepted congratulations from well-wishers. There were many people who came to shake her hand, wish her well, and view the famous barrel. Accompanying her was a Captain Johnson, whose device made for strapping her in the barrel aided in saving her life. On display was the main part of the barrel, a bicycle pump to show how they had pumped additional oxygen into the barrel, and a black and white kitten, "Lagara," that had gone over the Falls in a trial run.[65] Lagara did fine; she survived the plunge over the Falls!

After all the fanfare in Buffalo, Annie went back to Auburn, New York. She did not come back to Niagara Falls until early April 1902, about six months after the attempt. After that she planned on returning to her home in Bay City, Michigan. Sadly, she believed her manager, Frank Russell, had absconded with her barrel, and he was rumored to have taken a young lady posing as Annie Taylor with him. Annie had hoped to take the actual barrel on a speaking tour. For whatever reason, she did not make it back to Bay City. She left sometime later to go to New York City for about a year.

In some ways Annie was ahead of her time in regard to marketing. She went to Orange, New Jersey with plans of having a moving picture made of her death-defying plunge over the Falls. While there she also had souvenir barrels manufactured to sell at her speaking engagements.

While Annie stayed in New York City she had several speaking engagements, but due to her poor speaking skills, and lack of stage presence, she received quite poor reviews.

She returned to the Falls area a year later, in 1903. Annie commissioned the J. B. Bishop Cooperage Company to construct another barrel, a duplicate of the original, to take on her "lecture tours."[66]

In 1904, along with her barrel, Annie gave lectures in towns such as Niagara Falls, Jamestown, Dunkirk, and Lockport. In the early winter of 1904 she also traveled East and South, lecturing at various department stores, where it's likely that she met friendlier audiences. Annie also had miniature replicas of her barrels made to sell for souvenirs.

* * * * *

The rest of her life was fairly well known. She tried to make a go of public speaking, touring, and telling about her great adventure. But, in reality, the public just couldn't accept a woman, an older woman at that, as a daredevil heroine in the early 1900s.[67] Her accomplishment of conquering the Falls in a barrel was ridiculed in the *Buffalo Times* as being of no more importance or skill than that of a cat that had been put in a bag and thrown over the Falls. The article was written by an anonymous columnist writing under a pseudonym. It was a cowardly jab at someone who, at the least, many people thought of as a hero.[68] In the *Gazette*, Annie was villainized as not being willing to pay a fair wage to the gentlemen who rowed her out to Grass Island. At that time the pay offered was a week's wages for just a few hours' work. Her manager, Russell, however, subsequently raised the wages, and the matter was properly taken care of.[69]

Nor was there appreciation for the genius in Annie's forethought and planning of a barrel that could take her safely over the Falls. In many ways, Annie was a figure born before her rightful time in history. Had she been born later, her end-of-life story would have played much differently. During her era, the public looked at her in a largely unaccepting and negative way.

In 1902 Annie wrote a book describing her great adventure, *Over the Falls*. She haunted the sidewalks of the small town of Niagara Falls, New York for many years, peddling her book to souvenir shops, tourists, and whoever would stop and listen to her story.[70]

Annie was penniless and homeless when she was admitted to the Niagara County Infirmary on March 4, 1921. She was also blind and suffering from depression. She passed on not quite two months later, on April 30, 1921.[71] She was 82 and had lived not quite twenty years after her Falls stunt.

A few friends of Annie's gathered up donations so she could be buried in Oakwood Cemetery, Niagara Falls, New York, just two days later, on May 2. (Other notable figures also have been buried in this cemetery.[72]) Annie's life ended on a sad note, but she accomplished many of the things she set out to do. In the face of disapproval and ridicule she did what many thought impossible. She had a hard life but made the best of it she could, especially at a time that was not kind or benevolent to women in her situation.

In her last moments, witnesses said, she spoke of her beloved husband Samuel and dear Cal. She said she would soon be holding her son again. As she faded away, she felt herself floating peacefully and looking back at the Falls—and this time she was smiling.

In Her Words: Annie's Trip Over the Falls

"(I) rode to the shore of the Upper Niagara in a closed carriage
. . .

"On October 24, 1901, on Thursday afternoon, I left a private house on First Street, Niagara Falls, New York, entered a closed carriage and was driven rapidly to the shore of the Upper Niagara. Here the reporters and a great many others had gathered to see me start and to say goodbye, but I said, 'No, I will not say goodbye, but au revoir. I will see you in fifty minutes, below the cataract.' I was, however, twenty-five minutes late. I entered a rowboat rowed by two rivermen. We were followed by two other men in another boat, one holding a line from the first boat. I was rowed out to Grass Island. This island lies one and one-half miles above the Horseshoe Falls. Here I sent the men away. I quickly divested myself of my hat, street coat, heavy outside skirt, and put my foot in the barrel and slid in by contracting my shoulders as much as possible. I did not say, like Dante, 'Who enters here leaves all hope behind.' My mind was perfectly free and every sense alert, and I felt I could fling myself like a rock into the sea. If so I could win my objective. The men returned quickly, sealed the barrel with a wrench, and started to row me into the current which was moving directly to the Horseshoe Falls.

> My mind was perfectly free and every sense alert, and I felt I could fling myself like a rock into the sea.

"I said to the men, 'When you cut the rope that holds the barrel, rap loudly on the barrel so I will know I am started on my way alone, for I am making a trip from which no traveler has ever returned.' Soon came the rap and the barrel glided smoothly away like a thing of life, fighting for its prey, dashed this way and that through mountains of spray until it came to the first declivity one-half mile above the falls. This is a drop of some forty feet, though from the shore it does not look over ten or fifteen feet. Here the iron on the foot of the barrel caught on a fragment of rock or driftwood. The barrel turned head down, gave a lurch, and then turned and plunged to the bottom of the river. Again I heard the iron on the foot of the barrel grind into the bed of the river as the waters closed over my head in a swish, but I was not hurt or frightened. The barrel rose instantly to the surface and pursued its way toward the Falls. Suddenly I felt it swerve toward the left. I knew instinctively that if it should be carried to the Canadian shore I would be instantly dashed to pieces on the rocks at the base of the Falls. It may sound strange, but still I was not frightened. I resigned myself to whatever fate had in store for me. I knew my motives were pure and exalted though my life were to pass.

"Then just as suddenly, the barrel paused in midstream, the foot lifted, and I felt myself being turned from side to side. Finally, the barrel righted itself and once again followed its course toward the mighty cataract. Now it entered the smooth swift current that makes its way around the bend in the river. For the first time I could hear the roar of the Falls sounding like continuous thunder.

"I tore a small cushion from my hand and placed it quickly under my knees. Then I clasped my hands tightly [yet] relaxing every muscle in my body. I dropped my head on my breast when I realized I was on the brink of the awful precipice. The barrel seemed to pause for one second. Then [swiftly] it made the awful plunge of one hundred and fifty-eight feet to the boiling waters far below. The sensation was one of indescribable horror. I felt as though all nature was being annihilated; there was no sensation of striking the waters in the lower river. [I] simply knew I was in the terrifying cauldron at the base of the Falls. I went down, far below the surface. Not a sound reached my ears. I felt alone, cold, and forsaken. No longer could I reckon time. It seemed about a minute. Perhaps it was much longer before the barrel started upward. It shot up from the depths with almost the same velocity I'd experienced going down. I think it must have shot up into the air some ten or fifteen feet. Then it came down again with a horrible plunge. Unfortunately, when it rose to

> The barrel seemed to pause for one second. Then [swiftly] it made the awful plunge of one hundred and fifty-eight feet to the boiling waters far below.

the surface the second time, the barrel came up under the water pouring over the precipice. Now I was carried back into what may have been a chasm or cave behind the cascading torrents. The barrel was picked up like a feather and dashed around in midair. Then it dropped on some rocks and whirled around with the greatest rapidity. It seemed as though it lifted and turned like the dasher in a great churn.

"Now my strength was fast giving way. I knew where I was but I still was not afraid. Suddenly an explosion of air sent the barrel out into what rivermen call the Maid of the Mist eddy. All at once I heard the barrel grate upon the rocks. It was [at] that instant I knew I was saved. My head dropped forward.

> It was then I fully realized I had just accomplished a feat no other person in the world had accomplished.

"I did not hear the men open the barrel, but when fresh air struck my face I heard a man exclaim, 'The woman is alive.'

"I answered, 'Yes, she is.' I raised my hand and two men lifted me to [a] plank. I remember I walked to the shore unaided. I was placed in a carriage and driven to the American side. I don't recall anything about going through customs. I could hear the bells ringing and whistles blowing. It was then I fully realized I had just accomplished a feat no other person in the world had accomplished.

"Men surrounded the carriage, detached the horses, and drew the carriage to the house. They wanted to lift me to their shoulders and carry me. I was almost overcome and begged them to let me go quietly."

Annie's Life and Travels

1. Early life of Annie Taylor: born (per her, 1855), speculated by others as 1838

   a. Married to Samuel D. Taylor at the age of 18. Date unknown. Married for a short time, lost a child, and her husband through death.

   b. Attended and graduated from the Normal State School at Albany, New York—either 1879 or 1880

2. In 1880 and beyond Annie went on her first extensive travels. First went by ship to Cuba for one or two months.

   a. Then by ship to Galveston, Texas

   b. By railroad to Austin, Texas

   c. By stagecoach to San Antonio, Texas

   d. She taught high school in San Antonio

   e. Took a vacation in New Mexico (where her party was in jeopardy of attack by a Native American tribe); they were under the protection of a Captain Nolan

f. Went back to San Antonio. Later that year she was robbed and chloroformed where she was staying; $3,000 was stolen from her.

g. On her return trip to New York, she was traveling by stagecoach between San Antonio and Austin when the coach was held up by a gang of robbers. All the other passengers were male; all were made to give up their valuables and cash. Annie escaped this, though, hiding her cash in her dress.

3. Career moves

a. Annie next traveled to New York City for dance instruction for one year.

b. She went next to Chattanooga, Tennessee, where she was burned out of her boarding house. She also lost $1,700 in bad investments to a swindler who skipped town.

c. Next: Asheville, North Carolina, where she taught dance and physical culture for a summer.

d. Just after that time she traveled to Charleston, South Carolina and was there during the famous Aug. 31, 1886 earthquake.

e. Spent the next winter teaching in Washington, D.C.

f. Next to Auburn, New York, where she stayed for the summer and autumn (likely with a friend, sister, or relative; in this book I speculate she stayed with a good friend).

g. Next she took a job in Lafayette, Indiana, where she taught dancing at a Young Ladies School.

h. She spent some time in Bay City, Michigan.

i. Next: Sault Ste. Marie, Michigan, where she taught piano music.

j. Next: travels back to San Antonio.

k. From there: Mexico City, Mexico, where she spent the month of December for the Christmas holidays of 1888.

l. Returned to San Antonio for a brief time.

m. The next spring Annie went back to Bay City, Michigan to teach classes in physical culture. She lived in Bay City until October 4, 1901, when she traveled to Niagara Falls for her famous Falls attempt. Her purpose in the attempt was to help two friends in debt, and she also was in debt. (She needed to sell her land in Texas as well.)

4. The Falls attempt: October 1901

a. Niagara Falls: After moving there on October 4, it was on October 24, 1901 (her birthday) that she went over the Falls in a well-publicized stunt—and lived to tell about it.

b. Did speaking engagements and traveled some after her attempt. Spent time between Auburn, New York, and Niagara Falls.

5. Final years

    a. For her last decade and a half, she was based mostly in Niagara Falls, New York. Did some speaking and worked to sell her book and souvenirs.

    b. On April 30, 1921, destitute and being cared for at an infirmary as a charity patient, Annie Taylor passed away. (She had been taken into the home only in early March.)

    c. Friends raised money to have her buried in Oakwood Cemetery in Niagara Falls, New York.

Annie's Tenure as a Normal Student Teacher

In the 1820s and 1830s common schools became prevalent in the cities and rural towns of the United States. But there was a problem that first had to be addressed: who would train the teachers for these schools? Most common school teachers had minimal training, and many were only educated at the common school level. Teaching tenures were often short—men usually taught only until they found a higher-paying job, and women only taught until they married. For true improvements in education, more progress was needed.

In 1832, the state of Massachusetts began its first normal school, a school for the express purpose of training teachers. The school proved to be a success, and by 1844 the state had three normal schools, albeit small ones.

Government officials and educators in New York State saw the success of Massachusetts and decided to experiment with a larger school in their state. The Albany Normal School opened in 1844 in a refurbished railroad depot. Part of the reason it was located in the state capital of Albany was so that the state government could watch over its experiment. The school was a success, and by 1848 it was granted permanent funding. The school grew rapidly in size, to nearly 250 students, a number equal to all three Massachusetts schools combined. In 1849 the school moved to a brand-new building in downtown Albany. The building had separate entrances for men and women, reflecting the customs of the times.

Students came from throughout the state, and a majority were men. Many would be considered what today are called non-traditional students. Many new students had already taught in the common schools and came to the Albany Normal School to solidify their teaching skills. Others came from rural areas of western New York where there were few schools of higher education, and the Albany Normal School was the only opportunity for many of them to get an extended education.

The school continued to prosper, and the state opened other normal schools. Only a small percentage of students ever graduated from the two-year program, however, as many left to take teaching positions before their graduation. Some graduates would teach for many years, and some became principals or went west to found other normal schools. Some never taught, instead returning to the family farm or choosing another profession. Several Albany Normal School graduates became lawyers, doctors, and ministers.

Education and knowledge became important cornerstones of the United States after the American Revolution. Knowledge for the common citizen was an important ideal of the new republic and an essential feature to its continuance. Early in the nineteenth century, people began to realize that the best way to educate the public was with free public schools. Before this, most teachers taught privately or in academies, usually available to only the wealthy citizens.

Source: http://www.albany.edu/faculty/aballard/civilwar/
normalschool.htm (accessed May 1, 2020)

BIBLIOGRAPHY

Taylor, A. E., *Over the Falls* (1902).

Parish, C.C., *Queen of the Mist* (Interlaken, New York: Heart of the Lakes Publishing, 1987); several sections researched and quoted from the "Cataract Journal at Niagara Falls."

Wikipedia, "Annie Edson Taylor." Retrieved from https://en.wikipedia.org/wiki/Annie-Edson-Taylor

Find A Grave Memorial #127712354, 2014.

Ancestry.com, 2019

Brockway, C., *Images of America: Newark* (Charleston, S.C.: Arcadia Publishing, 2004), p. 112.

The Guardian.comworld, Michigan-lake-huron-shipwreck-marine sanctuary-thunder-bay-expanded. Accessed at https//www.theguardian.comworld/2014/sep/05/.

Handbook of Texas, Gambling-in-the-old west. Accessed at http://www.historynet.com, p. 17.

Wilkinson ranch. Retrieved from blog.wilkinsonranch.com/2013/08/07/then-and-now congress-avenue-austin-texas, accessed June 23, 2015.

Wikipedia: Austin, Texas. Accessed at Https://en.wikipedia.org/w/index.php?title=Austin,-Texas&printable.

Texas Almanac: stagecoaching. Retrieved from http://texasalmanac.com/topics/history/stagecoaching-texas, accessed June 28, 2015.

Buffalo Library: Pan-am. Retrieved from http://library.buffalo.edu/pan-am/, accessed April 12, 2015.

New York Times, 1880. Accessed at https://www.nytimes.com/books/first/s/ster-1880.html, multiple paragraphs, accessed October 30, 2015.

Legends of America. Accessed at https://www.legends of America.com/picuewpages/PP.SaloonDecor-9.html.

Ephemeral New York (2015). Gilded Age New York, accessed at https://ephemeralnewyork.wordpress.com/tag/gilded-new-york/

New York Times. Accessed at https://www.nytimes.com/gooks/first/s/ster-1880.html pg7, accessed October 30, 2015.

Musicals 101. Retrieved from https://www.musicals101.com/1880s.htm, p. 2.

WCU.edu (1890). Retrieved from http://www.wcu.edu/library/Digital Collections/TraveWNC/1890s/180asheville.html.

Wikipedia (2016), Charleston. Retrieved from https://en.wikipedia.org/wiki/Charleston.

Wikipedia (2016), Washington, D.C. Retrieved from https://en.wikipeida.org/wiki/History of Washington, D.C.

US Army Corps of Engineers, Detroit District.

Mexico City Attractions. Teotihuacan Pyramids. Retrieved from http://www.viator.com/Mexico-City-attractions/Teotihuacan-Pyramids/d628-a1760.

Wikipedia (2016), Christmas in Mexico. Retrieved from https://en.wikipeida.org/w/index.php?title=Christmas in Mexico&oldid=714358432.

http://texasalmanac.com/topics/history/stagecoaching-texas, accessed on June 28.

https://www.mnn.com/green-tech/transportation/stories/ how-fast-could-you-travel-across-the-us-in-the-1800s, accessed on 12/01/2017.

Handbook of Texas Online, T. R. Fehrenbach, "San Antonio, Texas".

Houstonculture.org/Hispanic/roads.html; authors: Morales and Schmal.

Find A Grave, 2018: https://www.familysearch.org/tree/ person/details/LVJVCG2.

NOTES

(See Bibliography for full detail on many of these sources.)

1 Find a Grave.

2 Find a Grave.

3 Taylor, A. E., *Over the Falls* (1902), p. 6.

4 Taylor, A. E., *Over the Falls* (1902), p. 5.

5 Taylor, A. E., *Over the Falls* (1902), p. 5.

6 Taylor, A. E., *Over the Falls* (1902), p. 5.

7 Find A Grave Memorial #127712354, 2014.

8 Taylor, A. E., *Over the Falls* (1902), p. 6.

9 Wikipedia, "Annie Edson Taylor." Retrieved from https://en.wikipedia.org/wiki/Annie-Edson-Taylor.

10 Find A Grave Memorial #127712354, 2014.

11 Ancestry.com, 2019.

12 Gettysburg.stonesentines.com/battle-of-gettysburg.facts/the-states.at-gettysburg/dtd 1/27/2019.

13 Find A Grave, 2018, https://www.familysearch.org/tree/person/details/LVJVCG2).

14 Taylor, *Over the Falls.*

15 Ibid.

16 Ibid.

17 Ibid.

18 Ibid.

19 Ibid.

20 Ibid.

21 http://www.historynet.com/gambling-in-the-old-west.htm. Accesssed April 15, 2015.

22 Handbook of Texas online, p. 17, para 1.

23 Blog.wilkinsonranch.com/2013/08/07; accessed June 23, 2015.

24 https://en.wikipedia.org/w/index.php?title=Austin,Texas; accessed June 23, 2015.

25 http://texasalmanac.com/topics/history/stagecoaching-texas; accessed June 28, 2015.

26 en.wikipedia.org/wiki/New_Braunfels_Texas; accessed Nov. 3, 2017.

27 Ibid.

28 Parish, C.C., *Queen of the Mist.*

29 Taylor, *Over the Falls.*

30 Ibid.

31 Ibid.

32 Brockway, C. *Images of America: Newark* (Charleston, S.C.: Arcadia Publishing, 2004).

33 http://library.buffalo.edu/pan-am/; accessed April 12, 2015.

34 Ibid.

35 https://www.nytimes.com/books/first/s/ster-1880.html; accessed October 30, 2015.38 Ibid.

36 Ibid.

37 Ibid.

38 Ibid.

39 www.maggieblanck.com/New York/Life.html.

40 Ibid.

41 http://www.wcu.edu/library/DigitalCollections/ TravelWNC/1890 /1890asheville.html; accessed January 4, 2016.

42 https://en.wikipedia.org/wiki/Charleston-South-Carolina; accessed January 14, 2016.

43 http://www.wcu.edu/library/DigitalCollections/ TravelWNC/1890 /1890asheville.html; accessed January 4, 2016.

44 https//en.wikipeida.org/wiki/History_of Washington, D.C.; accessed January 22, 2016.

45 Ibid.

46 Ibid.

47 http:www.saultcity.com/historic-homes; accessed on May 1, 2017.

48 Taylor, *Over the Falls.*

49 https://www.mnn.com/green-tech/transportation/stories/ how-fast-could-you-travel-across-the-us-in-the-1800s; accessed December 1, 2017.

50 Handbook of Texas Online, T. R. Fehrenbach, "San Antonio, TX"; accessed December 1, 2017.

51 Legends of America.com/TX-mengerhotel.html; accessed December 1, 2017.

52 http://www.mexconnect.com/articles/2-mixican-history-a-brief-summary; accessed February 3, 2016.

53 Legends of America.com/TX-mengerhotel.html.

54 https://www.britannica.com/biography/Porfirio-Diaz ; accessed June 1, 2020.

55 https://en.wikipedia.org/w/index.php?title=Christmas_in_Mexico&oldid=714358432; accessed July 31, 2016.

56 Ibid.

57 http://www.viator.com/Mexico-City-attractions/Teotihuacan-Pyramids/d628-a1760; accessed February 3, 2016.

58 https://en.wikipedia.org/w/index.php?title=Christmas_in_Mexico&oldid=714358432.

59 https://en.wikipedia.org/wiki/Texas_Mexican_Railway ; accessed June 1, 2020.

60. https://www.baycitymi.org/150/History-of-Bay-City.

61 Taylor, *Over the Falls.*

62 Taylor, *Over the Falls.*

63 Ibid.

64 Parish, C.C., *Queen of the Mist.*

65 Ibid.

66 Ibid.

67 Ibid.

68 Ibid.

69 Ibid.

70 Ibid.

71 Ibid.

72 Ibid.